I0665497

stop requested

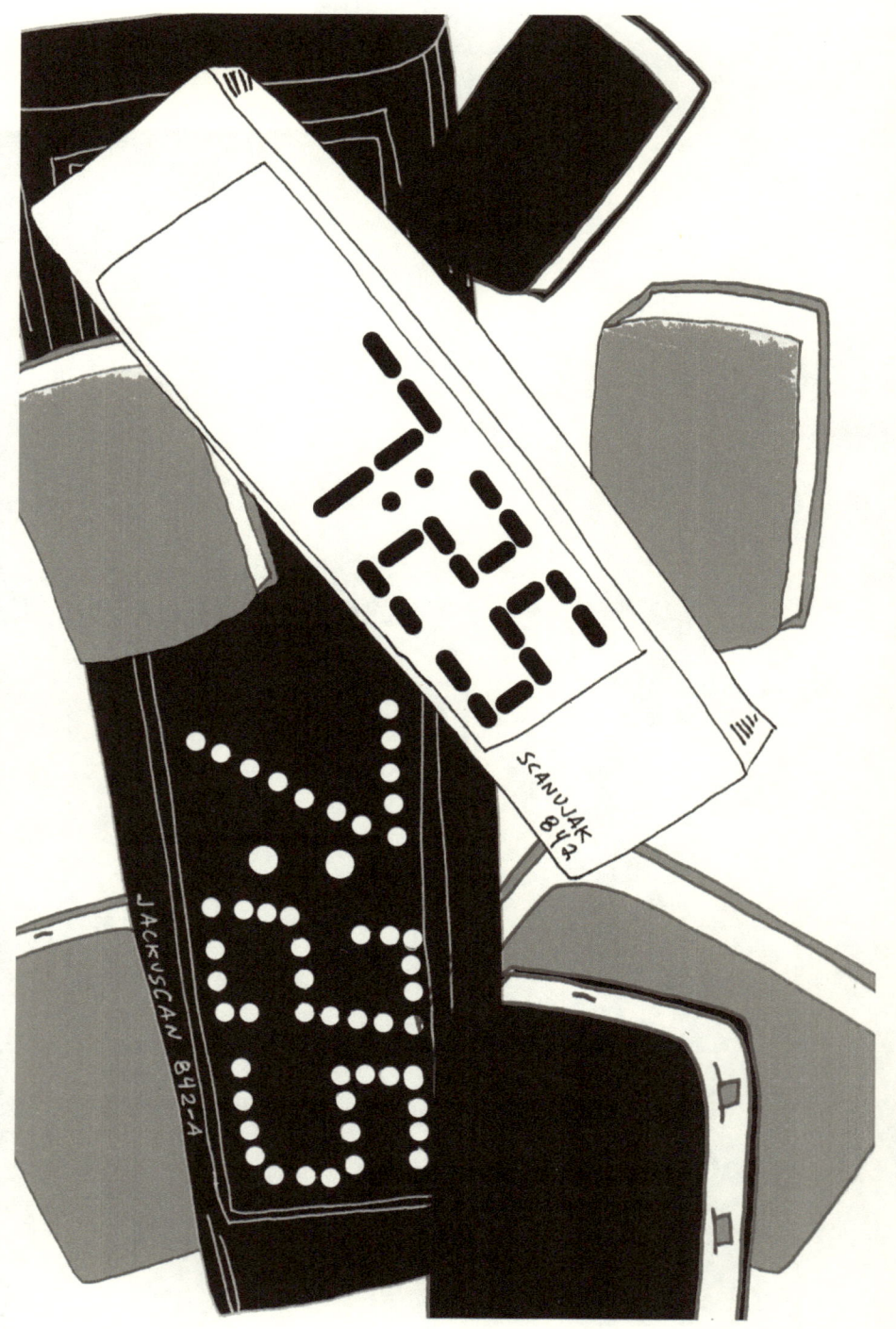

Wyatt Doyle

stop
requested

Illustrations by Stanley J. Zappa

new texture

If you enjoy this book, tell someone about it.

A New Texture book

Text copyright © 2010 by Wyatt Doyle
Illustrations copyright © 2010 by Stanley J. Zappa

All Rights Reserved.

Cover by Stanley J. Zappa & Wyatt Doyle

Copy editor: Sandee Curry / www.SandeeCurry.com
Book design and layout by Wyatt Doyle

Several of these stories appeared on the NewTexture.com website
in different form and are included here by permission.

www.NewTexture.com

Booksellers: *Stop Requested* and other New Texture books are
available through Ingram Book Company

ISBN 978-0-9827239-0-6

First New Texture Edition: June 2010
Printed in the United States

10 9 8 7 6 5 4 3 2 1

FOR MOM AND DAD
I'm very lucky.

contents

bumpier than usual

THE 842 is a bus about half the size of the average city model. If you've ever been in an airport shuttle, one of the small ones, it's the same thing. They call it a "cutaway." It runs on Laurel Canyon from Studio City to West Hollywood and back again. If everybody squeezes, it seats about twenty.

Laurel Canyon is a hilly, winding route, and bumpy besides. And while the rickety 842 handles the terrain with all the grace and stability of a Model T, other than the clanking and thudding of the bus itself, it's usually a pretty quiet ride.

Taking the same route on the same schedule, week in and week out, in what is essentially an oversized van, you develop at least a nodding acquaintance with your fellow passengers. Even the Korean grandfather at the wheel is just one of the gang; some of the regulars call him "Uncle Pete"—though another driver told me his name was actually Albert.

Last night the usual crowd was joined by a troubled young white guy wearing headphones, his hair uneven in a cancer patient crew cut of tufts and patches. He stood apart from the group, calling out to an audience in his head. Only occasional snatches of his shouting were audible over the passing traffic.

"...I'm the son of a Satan worshipper, that's what's going on! It's like *The Twilight Zone*. This entire nation is working to try to make me crazy, making me say I like the terrorists!"

He shivered.

"Yeah, you said I was no good at that, that my dick wasn't shit. You like those black guys, with their big thing hanging down their legs...."

Nearby, oblivious to the ranting, a tall, bald black man in a dark blue ninety-nine dollar suit blasted a cassette of Chaka Khan's *Greatest Hits* from a portable tape deck, using his thumb to thump out bass lines on the radio's plastic shell.

Twilight Zone quieted down when the bus pulled up, and as we loaded in, he joined us like any other working stiff on his way home. There were more black men than usual on the bus, and anyone wondering how their presence—particularly in such close quarters—might affect his testimony wasn't kept in suspense.

"Yeah, you all think these white women want you," he continued brazenly. "They don't want you! They just fuck you to keep you from *rioting*! So you can hold your head up *high*!"

An older black man sat near the front, a pint bottle poking out of his back pocket. Dressed in pinstripe trousers long retired from formal occasions, a thin leather jacket from the '80s and a sweatshirt sporting a cracked and faded logo for The Laugh Factory comedy club. He frowned at Twilight Zone's tirade, and called across the aisle to the young black professional seated next to me.

"You hear what this white boy said about you?!"

My neighbor took out iPod earbuds and plugged them into his head.

"Uh huh. You'll take it from him, but you wouldn't take it from me! Yeah, put your headphones on. You wouldn't take it from *me*!"

Laugh Factory wasn't a big man, but in small spaces, being drunk and loud takes on added dimension. Even Twilight Zone was a little surprised at the older man's outburst.

"It's all right, man," Twilight Zone assured him with a sudden gentleness. "I'm a drinker, too."

It was the last corner Laugh Factory was looking for

support from. His eyes locked on the white boy, and he pushed a hand into his jacket pocket as though reaching for something.

"One more word out of you...." he told Twilight Zone ominously. "I just did seven years for taking care of some motherfucker *just like you*!"

"I—"

"One more word! I'll take care of you right here! ONE MORE WORD! NOT ANOTHER FUCKIN' WORD!"

For a moment, no one said anything. In the silence, Laugh Factory calmed down.

"I'm not mad at you," he said at last, waving his dismissal. "I'm not mad at anybody. I don't care if you're black, white, green or purple. We all on the bus. We all *poor* here. We all trying to make something better than what we got."

He sighed.

"I got twelve dollars in my pocket. What good is *twelve dollars* gonna do you?"

He sat back, calmer, and took a deep breath. Then he leaned forward, happy, his hands on his knees as his face bloomed into a satisfied expression.

"It's my *birthday* today. I bet you people didn't know that. I'm seventy-three years old!" All things considered, he looked great for seventy-three. Perhaps to commemorate the occasion, he launched into a number from the Philly Soul jukebox in his head:

"FAAAMILY... REUUUUNION! FAAAAMILY! REUUUNION!"

He very well may have been making it up as he went, but he sang passionately at the top of his voice what must have been the entire song, rhyming *"laughter, love and tears"* with *"all these many years."* He wailed sentimental lyrics about *"coming together for the first time...in a long time,"* before sailing off into an absurd, prolonged falsetto on the fade.

Then he passed out.

A few stops later, at Santa Monica and Fairfax, Twilight Zone stood and exited quietly, so as not to wake the old man sleeping soundly by the door.

man down

ON MY last bus home, there is a woman who dresses only
in pink. She is blonde and slight, and pale pink is it for
her. Pink skirt, pink denim jacket, pink boots. It's like the
old joke: *Any color you like, so long as it's pink.* That's her.
Every day. Always. She's a regular.

Anya is a regular, too. She's Russian, from Belarus.
She's young, and smart-girl pretty. She tends to keep
to herself, though as fellow regulars, she always very
graciously says hello.

The 842 isn't much of a cruising spot, and I'd only ever
seen two guys try to pick her up. One was a gregarious and
chatty 12th grader; he said he was 22, but he was just tall.
He didn't discourage easily, but he didn't get anywhere
either.

The other was a 30-something guy in glasses. He was
short and average-looking, but he put out a cocky vibe and
came off as hostile and defensive. The type who'd spent
most of his life being picked on, or at least feeling he was,
and he'd spend the rest of it smoldering for payback. He
wore it all over.

Yet he was the only one able to make any real time with
her. Last I'd seen, things had been getting cozier between
them, but when I didn't run into either of them for a while,
I didn't give it much thought.

A few weeks later when I did see them, they were seated
silently next to each other on the bench at the stop. Once
they boarded the bus, they sat on opposite sides of the
aisle and didn't have much to say to one other. Whatever
first-date warmth existed between them had evaporated.
Probably he didn't move fast enough when he should
have, or maybe he moved too fast when he shouldn't have;
whatever it was hadn't been ugly, just awkward. And it
lingered. But both still had a bus to catch, and until one
of them changed their schedule, they remained riding
companions by default.

The woman in pink was on the day I saw them. She
passed on the way to her usual seat in the back, the

polyester fill of her ski jacket swooshing against itself as
she moved.

The guy made a few belated attempts to start a
conversation with Anya, sharing anecdotes about funny
things that happened at his workplace. But his stories
weren't funny, and the intended humor seemed lost on her
anyway. Mostly his job sounded boring. Soon he was quiet
again.

When the woman in pink passed them again to exit, he
tried another tack.

"That lady only ever wears pink," he said once she was
gone and safely out of earshot. "Never any other color. I've
probably seen her a hundred times, and that's the only color
she ever has on, pink. Just pink everything." He shook his
head.

She took a moment, considering her answer.

"Well," she said finally, "it's a nice color." She herself
had a pink jacket she wore when the weather was cooler.

He frowned. She didn't leave him any place to go.

He remained silent for the rest of the ride. As he got off
the bus, I noticed he was wearing cargo pants that could be
zipped off into shorts.

trying to get by

As THE bus I'm about to get off crosses the intersection, I see
my next one already stopped at the corner, waiting for the
light to change so it can leave without me. It's going to be
close, so I'm first out when we pull over and I race across
the street to intercept my connection. There are plenty
already riding, and a crowd waiting to board besides; that
means the buses on the route are either running late or not
showing up. It happens all the time.

I make it to the stop and get on line, stepping around
a big piece of luggage parked upright on the curb. Inside
the bus, a balding, bearded black man with freckles is
concluding a quick conference with the driver. Holding his
camouflage fishing hat down on his head, he emerges from
the bus and pushes past the line of boarding commuters. He
runs to the bag, then struggles to lift it through the open
back door.

The bus is full, so I walk to the back, where the seats
horseshoe around the rear wall. I take the middle seat, a
spot that for some reason is always empty. At the window to
my left, a Mexican guy with a moustache stares out at the
street; Freckles ends up seated at the window on the right.
He's laid his heavy bag down across several seats on the
side row in front of him. Freckles smells a little ripe, but it's
not that big a deal.

A burly white guy in flannel approaches from the front,
looking for an open spot. Seeing there isn't much available,
he takes hold of the ceiling rail and stands.

Freckles notices him and moves to take a firm grasp on
his valise.

"Hey man," he calls out, "would you like to sit down
here? I'll move my bag." The guy waves him off—"that's all
right"—but Freckles is determined to oblige him. He turns
to me. "I need to put my bag down here," he says. I move as
far as I'm able to one side for a moment, half out of my seat,
thinking he intends to somehow wedge it into the space
where he's sitting.

Instead, he yanks the bag off the seat and sets it down

square in the middle of the aisle, where it sits jammed against my leg. I wait for him to move it, but he settles in and shows no sign of moving anything. I push against it, but not too aggressively.

"You gotta move your bag, man," I tell him.

He jumps up from his seat and puts a hand on the luggage.

"Don't touch my bag! That's my stuff—don't you touch it! I don't want you messing with my stuff!" It's like I've not only offended him, but the dignity of all men everywhere.

"I'm homeless!" he chastises me. "I'm just trying to get by! That's everything I own right there. Don't you even think about touching my stuff."

"Then move it. I don't need your stuff touching *me*," I say, figuring we can all play princess.

He glares at me, keeping one hand on the upright bag as if protecting it. "I made sure I brought it in through the back door so I wouldn't bump anybody, wouldn't bother anyone, and I need to keep a hand on it.

"Slavery is *over*," he booms. He sits down, still glaring. "Touch my bag…. I'm *homeless*! I'm trying to get *by*!"

Freckles nods in the direction of a lone empty seat by the window on the other side of the aisle, in front of the Mexican guy.

"Why don't you sit over there?" he asks, exasperated.

"I've got a seat," I tell him.

"There's a empty seat right there! You can sit in that one."

"This is where I'm sitting." Screw this guy.

He exhales heavily, trying to contain his frustration. He reaches over and puts his hand on the grip of the bag's extendable handle, drawing it out then bringing it down like the plunger on a detonator, with a sharp, clean click. His fingers linger on the handle, as if the luggage needs steadying. Or maybe he's just savoring the fantasy of having explosives so close at hand. Gently patting the sides of the bag, he tries another tack.

"I got a big snake in here. I don't want him to get out," he mumbles, checking me for a reaction out of the corner of his eye. Meanwhile, no one has moved to fill the short row of seats he's cleared.

"Hey man," he calls out again to the man in flannel.

"You sure you don't want this seat here? I moved my bag."
The guy tells him he's fine where he is.

"Okay," Freckles says, standing up, "Since he doesn't
want to sit here, I'm going to move this bag back up on
these seats, so it won't be in your way."

"I appreciate it," I say, thinking he's extending an olive
branch. He isn't.

"Yeah, you appreciate it. You should appreciate that
slavery is *over*! You want to mix it up, go ahead. You can
mix it up with me, I ain't afraid. Touch my stuff…. You'll
go home to your wife, she'll know. She'll know you been
touched by somebody!"

He's fidgeting, I figure at least partly because he's not
entirely sure he can cash these checks he's writing.

Once he gets settled, he takes off his camo hat and sets
it on top of the bag. Then he changes his mind and puts
the hat back on. He reaches into a large side pocket where
he's keeping a fat-bodied quart bottle in a wrinkled brown
bag; he unscrews the cap and takes a good long slug before
zipping it back away. Then it's off with the hat again as he
takes out a pair of FM radio headphones.

"Slavery is over," he repeats, trailing off as he adds,
"Your ancestors fucked with my ancestors!"

"…And now you and me are *both* riding the bus," I'd
tell him, but by then he's got his headphones on, loud
enough for me to hear the music. He begins to sing, but he's
singing a ballad and the tune coming from the headphones
is audibly an uptempo dance number. Before the song
ends, the headset comes off and his hat goes back on—and
then comes off again. Grandly, he throws a leg up over the
backs of the seats in front of him, but it's not a comfortable
position and he soon returns to sitting normally.

I can't help but feel all of this is for my benefit.

A stop or two later, he gets up and makes a grand
production of taking the bag down. He extracts the handle
and wheels his way to the back door, but pauses before he
gets off. He calls to the front of the bus, to the driver.

"Thank you, I'm sorry about disrespecting you before
when I got on, but I was being disrespected. I'm homeless
and trying to get by." Catching himself starting down a road
he doesn't want to revisit, he shakes it off and lowers his

head. "God bless you," he says to erase any hostility. "God bless everybody."

But he makes a point of not turning around to include me.

A FEW months later, I run into Freckles again. He's traded his luggage for a bicycle. He secures his ride to the rack on the nose of the bus and walks to the back, taking a seat facing mine. He doesn't remember me.

He sits down, then gets up to open the window next to him. Half a minute later he gets up again, shoving open the emergency exit hatch in the ceiling to ventilate things further.

"Excuse me, man," he says as he crosses me to take his seat. "I need to let in some air."

"Okay with me, I like the breeze," I tell him.

He sits back down, across from me.

"I have to open these windows because people want to breathe the Devil on you," he confides. "People you see on the street, people on the bus, they want to *breathe* on you, and that's the Devil. All the diseases...hepatitis! And people breathe at you, and lick their lips.... I don't want any of that. I want the air to come in and blow it all away. Everyone is gonna have their judgment on Judgment Day, and the scales are gonna show the good and the evil. But 'til then..."

I just nod.

"I'm homeless. You can see that. But I don't need to be out here. My family are good people. They'll help me and look after me. But I won't let them. I'm not ready to accept that right now. I don't like it, but that's the way it has to be. See, I have a broken heart. I lost my mother recently, and this is where I have to be while I heal my broken heart."

"I'm sorry about your mother."

"Thank you, thank you for saying that. My nephew is Ray Baker, the boxer. My name's Kenney Baker, I'm his uncle. Look, you can see it in my face." He takes off his cap so I can make a better study, but I can't tell if he looks like him or not.

"I was the one who taught him how to box, but then he got a lot better than me!"

"Ray Baker's pretty famous. You must be proud of him."

"I am. I am very proud of him. I have a good family, that's the most important thing. He was raised right, just like I was. I had good home training."

"Are you from the South?" I ask, *home training* being a little Dixie for North Hollywood.

"Yes I am," he says without hesitation. "I'm from South Carolina. My father had a farm there. We had pigs in the back and long, long fences."

"Sounds like a good life."

"It is. It is a good life. It's so peaceful there, you wouldn't believe it."

"What made you leave it for here?"

"I got mixed up with a girl. I followed her out here to be with her, but it was no good." He frowns and stops there; he doesn't want to talk about it.

"I have to heal this broken heart. I have to stop buying that beer, stop that drinking. Fix myself up. I know God will help me."

"You'll do it," I tell him.

"Yes I will," he agrees, then reaches out to shake my hand again.

"You know, everybody's gonna go up there to the ice cream party or down there to the barbeque. And they won't be throwing ribs around at that barbeque, you know? Anyway I don't want *my* ribs getting barbequed!"

"Amen," I say.

As his stop comes up, he asks me for two dollars, saying he needs it to take another bus somewhere. I give it to him.

the difference between sad and sick

FOR a while, the 158's 8:10 morning run proved a powerful magnet for local eccentrics and random strangeness that put most other bus routes to shame. Then after about a year, the timetable got moved ten minutes and the cast of characters that had come to define the run all fell away. It was a particularly inexplicable turn of events in that, despite the official adjustment, the bus continued to arrive every morning at 8:10.

Celia was one of the first casualties of the schedule change. She was an older black woman, tall and thin and usually so drunk so early that by the time we picked her up at 8:15, even stringing words into a coherent sentence required a supreme act of will—will she regularly failed to summon. One morning she boarded laughing so hard to herself she could barely stand up straight.

"You already celebratin'?" the driver asked her rhetorically.

She wasn't as obviously intoxicated as I'd seen her at other times, but when you spend as much time shellacked as she did, you don't necessarily need a fresh coat to hold your shine.

First she sat near the driver, then she moved into the empty seat next to me. She leaned in close.

"Can I ask you a question?" she wondered. That was how she began most conversations.

"Sure."

"I have a tradition with my nephew. He is twelve years old, and every day when he comes home from school, I call him with a joke before he does his homework. I want to make sure he'll get this joke, make sure a twelve-year-old will get it."

"Okay."

She breathed in and squared her shoulders.

"What's the difference between sad and sick?" she asked.

"What's the...?"

"The difference," she said slowly, "between *sad* and *sick*."

I shrugged.

"*Sad* is when a mother finds her son smoking. *Sick* is when it's because his daddy set him on *fire*. Ha ha ha ha ha ha!" She grimaced, unable to control her laughter as she rocked back and forth in her seat.

Only the day before, my brother had told me a joke that I thought was funnier (*I heard they made a movie about yo' momma takin' a shower:* Gorillas in the Mist), but I didn't share mine.

"I think he'll get it," I told her. "I think a twelve-year-old will get that."

Still laughing, she got off at the next stop and told me to have a nice day.

in america

HE'D left his bag on the seat, and when an elderly lady eager to rest her bones almost sat on it, he erupted as though she'd dumped hot coffee in his lap. He was a particularly annoying passenger, and when her aged bottom inadvertently grazed his bag, he became incensed, bellowing in outrage as he whipped the bag out from under her. Shocked by his sudden explosion, the old lady jumped a mile.

The man doing the yelling was a regular on the route. On the losing side of his 50s, he was fat, gray, bearded and sloppy, and usually looked like he could use a wash. His stomach strained against his shirt buttons, and the black velvet of his yarmulke was heavily flecked with dandruff.

Nevertheless, he was an unrepentant snob. He spoke with a measured, skeptical delivery that came across as condescending; at best, merely tolerant. Combined with his thick Yiddish inflection, much of what he said ended up sounding like insulting questions posed rhetorically. This was fitting, since he regularly sought to engage drivers and fellow riders in intellectual argument, regardless of whether they shared his passion for it. His favorite occupation was debate with strangers for its own sake.

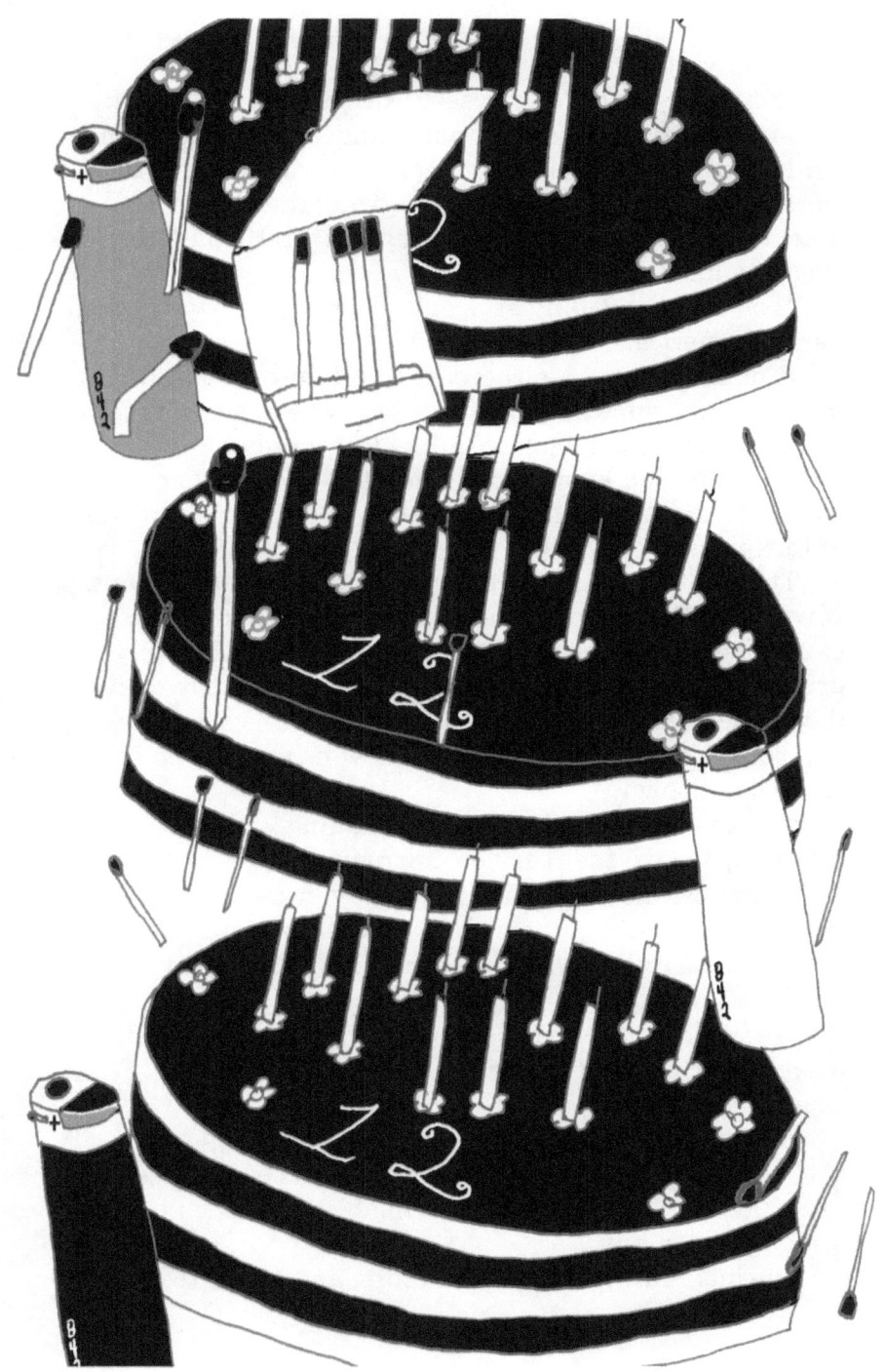

Sometimes they bit; mostly he fished.

But this was not an academic discussion, and the driver wasn't having it.

"You have to share your seat," he chastened. A black man in his 40s, he was reasonable and slow to anger. And while neither was a requirement of his profession, both were useful traits to have in it. Noticing the other man's accent, he mistook him for a recent arrival. He paused, choosing his words carefully.

"You can't be yelling at people. That's not how we do it here in America."

It might have ended there; after all, it was early morning—a time when most people on the bus don't even feel like talking, let alone arguing. But it didn't.

"What do you know about America?" the passenger snapped, absently thumbing a yellowed paperback edition of Euripides.

This wasn't a fight; it really wasn't even an argument. It was an exchange of challenges, a throwing down of gauntlets. There was no fury in either man's voice, only pride and a determination to have the last word, to deliver the inarguable summation. Neither had a hasty nature, and both felt this was one he should win. Their minor duel spooled out slowly.

The driver thought a moment. Leading with his chin, he raised his face to the rearview mirror.

"America," he called out in a steady, front-of-the-class voice, "is one nation, under God, indivisible, with liberty and justice for all. For all," he concluded. "Not just you."

"What is that?"

"You asked me what is America," the driver replied, pleased he'd thought to use the Pledge of Allegiance. "That's what I'm telling you."

His opponent sniffed.

"You think that's what America is? It is easy to fool you, I see," he purred, eyes never leaving his reading. "I have a bridge you can buy."

The bus continued along its route, and we all rode on.

imaginary friends

TRAFFIC was worse than usual, and like me, the 842 was running late. Everyone who should have been home on the previous run was still waiting at the stop when I got there.

It was like what people used to call "old home week," and I knew all the faces. In addition to the late afternoon regulars, I recognized some from the morning commute and others as infrequent travelers, special guests who only occasionally joined the party.

We packed into the tiny bus with several of us stuck standing as we barreled over the canyon. Two of the semi-regular cuckoos had managed to seat themselves facing one another across the aisle: the fat guy with acne who never changed his pants, and the Scribbler, a lanky crazy who always traveled with a full set of luggage.

The fat guy always gave off a sad feeling of bewildered displacement. He'd never really grown out of his awkward teenage years, and his inability to adapt to the outside world hung over him like a shroud. Scribbler, on the other hand, enjoyed no more success adjusting to the world around him, but didn't have time to think about it. He spent his travel time hunched over notes scratched frantically on scraps of paper, his bags forming a sacred circle that surrounded him like a wagon train.

I expected some stimulating discourse to develop between them, but none did. Scribbler occasionally offered jibes about current events to the bus at large, but the fat guy only watched him carefully, his face fixed in an enigmatic expression.

We passed a terrible car wreck in the opposite lane that had traffic at a standstill; this was the apparent cause of the bus delay.

Despite a head cold that was getting worse by the hour, I managed to catch a faint nose of the soothing jasmine that hung in the Laurel Canyon air that time of year. But it only lasted a moment, as the bus soon filled with a black, acrid chemical stench. When we didn't drive past it, I figured it had to be coming from us.

After a few minutes, one of the ladies called out grumpily, "Driver, could you turn on the air conditioning, please? It smells like burning rubber in here!"

"Brake pads," Scribbler announced without looking up from the paper he was writing on. "It's actually the smell of burning brake pads."

His correction did little to reassure his fellow passengers.

AT FAIRFAX, most of the crowd exited. From outside, someone asked the driver, "Do you go to Beverly?" When the driver acknowledged he did, a filthy bearded man in black sneakers and a lime green suit boarded.

"I don't have any money can I ride anyway thank you," he said as he hustled past the driver.

His dirty blue shirt was untucked, and the front flaps that hung over his crotch were stained a vivid, mustard yellow, a cartoon parody of a piss stain. It was almost theatrical.

A potato-faced woman too close to him in the boarding line scrunched her features in disgust. He took no notice and, despite the wide choice of seating options, chose the bench across from the Scribbler.

As the potato-faced woman passed him, the man in the green suit crossed his legs sharply, giving her shopping bag a good kick. He quickly apologized, but I preferred to think he was repaying her contempt.

Looking at the pair of lunatics facing each other, I was impressed that water had found its own level twice in one evening. Does madness exert a kind of magnetic attraction to its own? Do you recognize your peers and acknowledge them, the way drivers in the same make of car greet each other on the road?

Though they showed no outward sign of having met before, these two began conversing immediately. They didn't even look at one other, instead speaking off to the side in dull, flat tones as though addressing an imaginary friend, their statements trailing off into ellipses.

"Hey would you like to go get some coffee with me?" the filthy bearded man asked. "It would be all right if you want to go get some coffee with me...."

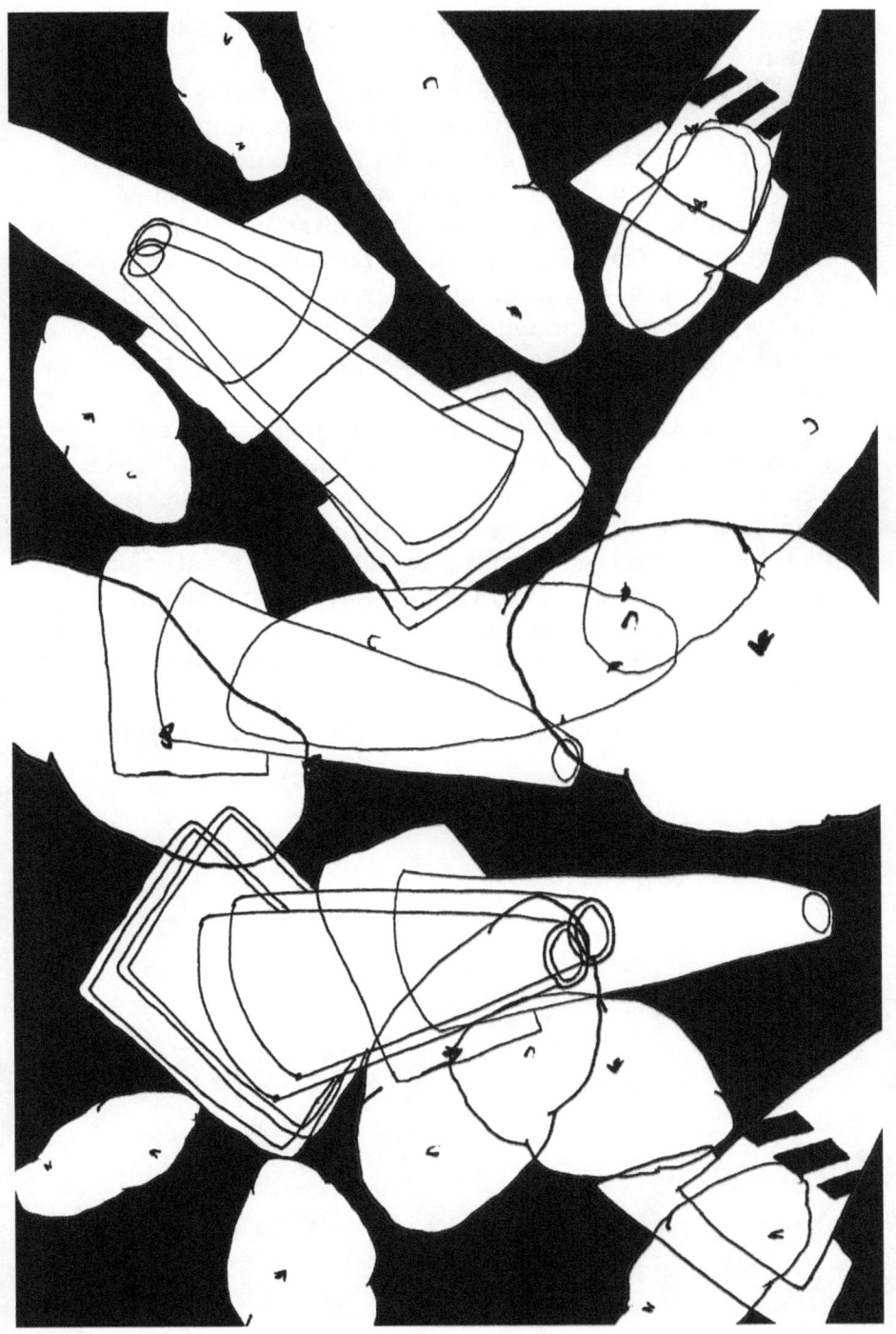

Still not looking up, Scribbler began to organize his notes. "There's a Starbucks right over that way, that's where I was going...."

"Well yeah I would like to get some coffee but I don't have any money. Uh I could get us two *cups* though..."

"Of course there is somewhere I have to go, first. There is a vitamin grocery called Open Lotus not far from here. First and foremost I have to go there, first and foremost. The founder of Open Lotus is a man named Ralph Flourpot. Ralph Flourpot who, when unwell, sought the advice of a Chinese herbalist and found the advice he received to be very helpful to his illness as well as general physical well-being...."

"Okay, what can you tell me about the contingency affidavit referring to the uh meretricious happenstance of the fuller requisite...." the dirty man responded quickly, raising the crazy bar. Scribbler matched him easily, talking over him with a lecture on the value of obscure nutritional supplements, several of which may have been fictional.

It all set my head spinning. Part of me wanted to stay on and listen, but there was no way I was going to be able to keep up.

Anyway it was my stop, and it really was time to go home.

no england

IT WAS late Saturday afternoon, and I was stuck waiting for the light to change while the 842 heading south idled at the stop across the street. The weekend schedule was infrequent at best, so I figured I'd better not miss it. I sprinted across the street at the first flash of green, managing to catch up to the driver's side window and startle her with a knock seconds before she would have pulled away.

"...Gonna get hisself *killed*," she was telling someone about me as I got on.

The small bus was packed. I joined those standing and grabbed a rail close to the ceiling. From the back, a very gay black man scolded me for my reckless approach to boarding.

"This isn't England!" he called.

AT FAIRFAX and Beverly, a very tiny old woman waited alone at the bus stop.

"You knew I was coming, so you baked a cake," she told the driver as she slowly climbed the stairs into the bus. The driver laughed.

Enough got off at the Farmers Market on 3rd that I could have a seat. Another elderly woman boarded, sitting across the aisle from the very tiny woman. Her hair was dyed a familiar shade of fried amber, and her clothes were festooned in loud, abstract patterns more suited to the dynamic upholstery of the 1970s, fitted in the loose, elastic-waistband style preferred by senior ladies. Though her fashion choices stood in dramatic contrast to the very tiny woman's short white hair and casual but conservative dress, they knew each other and were friendly.

"I like this bus," the flashier woman said. "I could take the other, but I prefer this one."

"Oh, I know," her friend concurred.

"Three stairs; this bus only has three stairs.... My legs have something wrong with them," she said by way of explanation.

"Oh!" she brightened. "But it was your birthday, wasn't it? How did that go?"

"It was fine," the other lady shrugged. "There were some problems."

"There were problems?"

"Well, *some* of the people drank five cups of coffee. And when I wouldn't give them more, they said"—she leaned forward and stage-whispered—"I was *prejudiced!*"

"They said that?"

She shook her head solemnly. "One cup of coffee is fine, maybe two."

"Or three," her friend added quickly, covering her own occasional indulgence.

"...But if I had to serve *everyone* five cups of coffee, I'd be *dead.*" She eased back into her seat. "...*And* there wouldn't be any more coffee!"

AN ODD-LOOKING woman near the front of the bus had been coughing most of the trip. She had a small, buggy face exaggerated by thick glasses, and she wore olive pants with a red jacket and a patch-patterned sweater. She had brooches pinned to both the jacket and the sweater, and there were old stains on her lapel that had dried white and were beginning to flake. She reached into the brown shopping bag at her feet and pulled out a package of prunes, examining them a moment before returning them to the bag; they appeared to be the only thing in there. She coughed again, grimacing with each spasm.

A younger man in a hooded sweatshirt who'd spent most of the ride seated in the back, his fingers pressed to his temples, suddenly rose, walked to the front and stood before her.

"This is a matter of religious principle for me," he explained, then reached out and placed a hand squarely on the woman's head.

"Lord Jesus, heal this woman, take the sickness from her. I can feel your sickness; I can feel it inside you. Jesus, this sickness is not a part of this woman, take it from her...."

A well-dressed old Russian man with a cane one seat

away took the younger man's arm.

"Enough," he told him through a thick accent. "Enough."

The younger man ceased his incantations and released his grip on the woman's head.

"You have to have faith," he announced dramatically to everyone as he returned to the back of the bus. "You'll see. She will be healed!"

The woman looked at the old man. She seemed confused, but not openly distressed. She put a hand to her head where the younger man had his moments before, and the old man murmured something to her in Russian.

A minute later, she coughed again.

My stop was next. The trip had not taken more than fifteen minutes. Twenty at most.

ain't gonna come 'til I'm ready

SATURDAY had turned to Sunday without fanfare a few hours earlier, and I was on Fairfax at Wilshire, waiting to catch the 217 heading north. I had no idea what time the bus was supposed to arrive, and there were three other men already waiting when I got there. It seemed unusual for that late hour.

One of them was a short, nerdy guy in full cycling gear. He stood by his bike, a schedule for every bus in the fleet tucked away in his backpack. He was taking great satisfaction in periodically complaining that the bus should have been there by then, periodically announcing that it was now running x minutes late.

"Probably it just isn't coming."

He was someone inexplicably determined to hold a conversation with anyone who would take the bait, a slave to a compulsion to let no quiet moment pass uninterrupted—even at a lonely bus stop in the middle of the night.

"The next one is due in fifteen minutes. If it even comes."

No one said anything.

"Well, we'd better hope the next one comes," he went on, "because the next one after that doesn't come for an hour." He looked down the wide, empty street. "Must be the traffic," he joked, but no one laughed.

A few minutes later, the bus wheezed into view. The bicycle guy was the last one on, and was still feeling scrappy.

"Can I ask you something?" he grilled the driver. "What was the holdup? We've been waiting for forty minutes. Two buses should have come by now." He tried his joke again: "Is it the traffic this time of night?" he snorted, but his joke didn't find an audience the second time around either.

"Sunset," the driver offered as catch-all explanation. Sunset Boulevard was a few miles away and in the opposite direction he was coming from, and he said it with the same flat tone people use when they say *you can't get there from here.*

The bicycle guy shook his head and started to walk to a seat, then returned to the driver.

"It's just that we were waiting out there freezing our asses off," he whined in what could safely be called an exaggeration of the truth. "And then no bus comes for forty minutes." Again, he moved to take his place among the passengers.

"Maybe next time I won't come at all, this is the gratitude," the driver called.

The bicycle guy turned once more and went back to the driver.

"Let me ask you something—do *you* ever take the bus?"

The driver stinkeyed him.

"All night long," he answered frostily.

This time the bicycle guy found a seat and took it.

"Maybe next time I won't come at all," the driver said again.

THERE was a small crowd waiting at the Farmers Market on 3rd. First to board was a woman in her 50s, a plump earth mother still holding down her end of the blissed-out California vibe of the 1970s. She carried a canvas bag that had a drawing of Kerouac and the name of a chain bookstore, and she picked a spot across from me, smiling beatifically.

Outside, two men about her age struggled to load a

bicycle onto the rack on the front of the bus. The portlier of the two stayed behind, waving goodbye from the curb. His friend boarded and positioned himself near the woman. He threw an arm over the back of the bench seat they shared— but definitely not around her shoulders.

"He's a nice guy. An interesting guy," he said, and she agreed.

"You know, he's a writer," he told her. "He could maybe help you with your stories."

"Yeah, but I don't need help with my stories." She wasn't defensive about it.

"Well, if you wanted, he said he goes to Barnes & Noble every Saturday." He gave her a lingering look. "I bet you have a lot of good stories."

"I do, but everyone has good stories." They fell silent, and she changed the subject.

"I was up late the other evening, and I saw that show Oprah, and she had Lance Armstrong on. Do you know who that is?"

"Oh, sure I do," he said. "He's wonderful. He was on with what's her name...."

"Sheryl Crow. I love Lance."

"She's much older than he is."

"She's not that much older!" she insisted.

"She's forty-one. He's thirty-three. It won't last."

"I think she's very pretty."

"No, she's attractive. But she's forty-one; he's only thirty-three. When men turn fifty, they start wanting something different."

"When they turn fifty?"

"Yeah, that's when they want something different."

She didn't respond.

"You look great," he transitioned awkwardly. "I mean, you don't look your age at all."

If she was flattered, it didn't show.

"I bet you've been married once before," he said.

"Once before?" she asked.

"Oh, more than once?"

"Several times," she said.

Rosewood was my stop. I made sure to thank the driver when I got off.

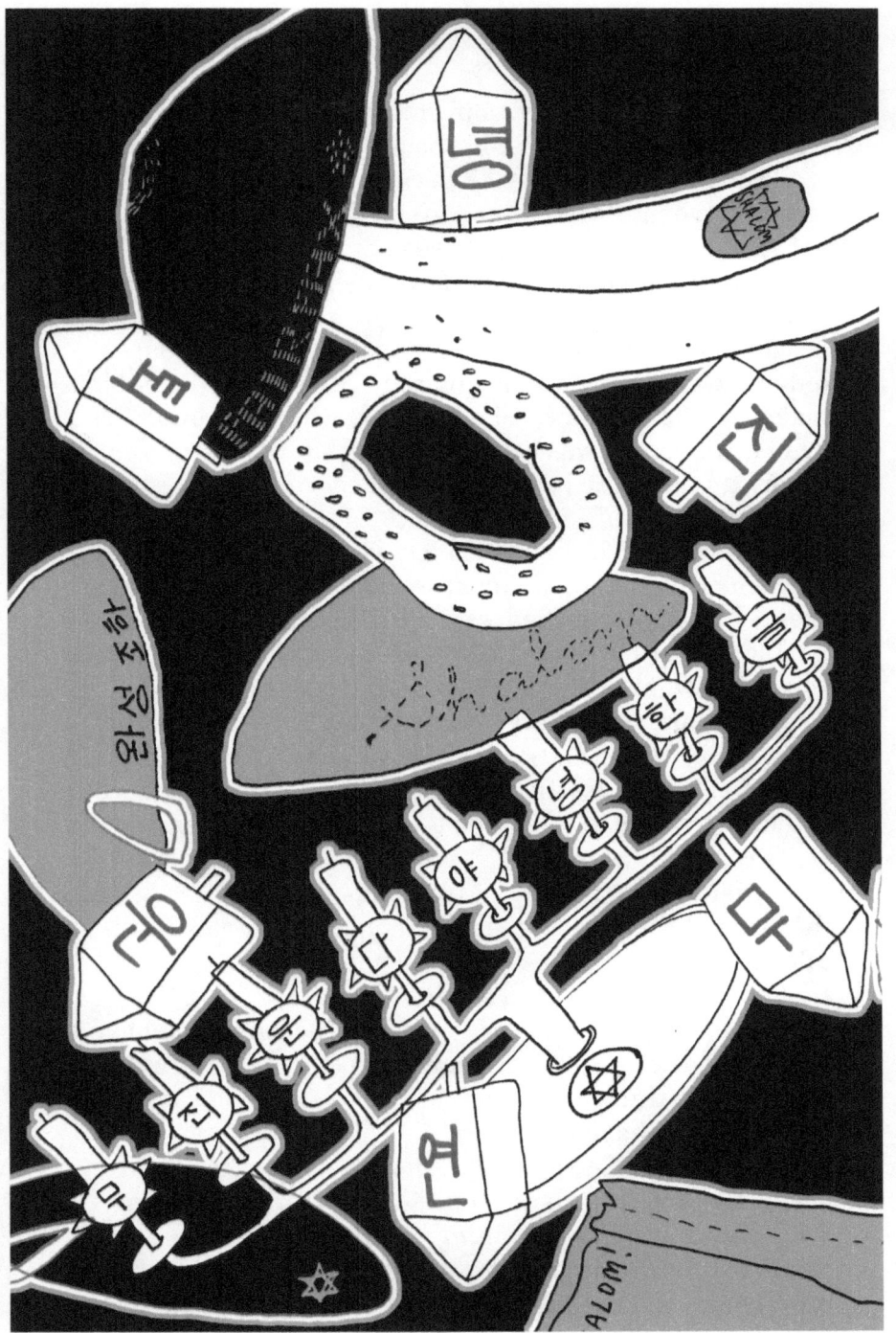

elegant balloons

FRIDAY the rain came down in chilly torrents, and Anya
from Belarus took shelter in the doorway of the drugstore
while she waited for the 842 to carry her home. She
emerged when it arrived and greeted me warmly. I let her
board ahead of me, and could see she was a bit wobbly
climbing the small stairway. I knew she'd been unwell, so I
asked how she was holding up.

"I am a little better, but I am feeling very unusual
today. I went to the doctor and they gave me medicine that
makes my head feel...." She moved her hands around her
head as though it was caught in a bubble. "I have never had
American medicine before," she sighed.

"It's stronger?"

"Yes! It's much stronger! I feel very high. I took some
in the morning, and all day at work it was as if I was in a
dream." She was amused, still a little stoned.

I looked at her more closely. Her pupils were so dilated
you could swim through one and back out the other.

"What are you taking?" I asked her. She looked at me
quizzically. "What is it called? Do you have it with you?"

"I don't have it with me. It's a syrup"—she pronounced
it the way you read it, sigh-RUP—"a cough syrup."

"From the drugstore?"

"I went to the hospital. My friends were worried because
they thought it was maybe pneumonia. But it was just a
cold."

"That must have been a relief."

"Yes, my friend was very worried. She said, 'You have to
go to the doctor!' But I don't have a doctor. I don't have...."
She couldn't think of the word.

"You don't have insurance?"

"Insurance!" She agreed. "I don't have insurance. My
friend took me to Cedars-Sinai, to the emergency room.
Well, *she* didn't. It was raining, and her friend likes to do
things for her, so *he* took me to the emergency room. He is
my friend, too. We had to wait two hours, and I had to leave
a deposit of three hundred dollars!"

"The emergency room is expensive."

"It is very expensive! They said they would send me a bill, and if it is less than three hundred dollars, they will return my money."

"Probably they will not return your money."

"I know. But I hope that it will not be *more* money. We had to wait all that time, and the doctor saw me for just five minutes!"

"Yeah, that's usually the way it works."

"My friend said they would pay the expenses, but I don't think they knew...." She shook her head, emphatically adding, "She *can't* pay three hundred dollars!"

"So you waited two hours to pay three hundred dollars for five minutes with a doctor who gave you drugs that are too much for you," I confirmed. "I would say you are having a very American experience. Have you been going to work all this time?"

"Yes. The doctor gave me a—I don't know what you would call it—a paper, excusing me from work. They said I need to rest. My friend who took me to the hospital made me promise to stay home, then the next day he called my work! But my boss said, 'She is already finished for the day,' so he knew I had been at work. Now I think my friend believes I disrespected him. But I don't think I disrespected him, do you?"

She leaned tipsily into the conversation like a girl a few drinks past her limit.

"He called your work? I don't know; calling you at work and talking to your boss seems a little extreme. You might even say he disrespected *you*, by calling your boss. That's not good."

"I know, I know. It is not good."

"Are you off tomorrow?"

"Tomorrow?" She had to think. "No."

"When are your days off?"

"Sunday. Sometimes Sunday."

"You have more than one job?"

"Yes. Sometimes I have to be at the restaurant Saturday and Sunday."

"You work six days a week, sometimes seven."

"Yes. But now I am working mostly one job."

"Six or seven days a week?"

"Sometimes fifty-six hours, sometimes sixty hours."

"At one job? You must make a lot of overtime."

It was a word she didn't know.

"Overtime," I repeated. "If you work over forty hours at any one place, you should make more money for the extra hours. Almost twice as much."

"Twice as much?" She was very surprised.

"You make what you would make for the hour, then half again. You don't make that?"

"No, I don't make double!" she laughed.

"Well, that's against the law."

"What law?" she laughed again, as if I were making it up.

"The law of the state of California! The law says he has to pay you extra for anything over forty hours."

"You don't understand, I went to *him* to ask for the extra work."

"That doesn't matter."

"We have an arrangement," she explained patiently. "Not an arrangement on paper, but I work these hours."

"Listen, a lot of people are in your same situation, but it is still against the law to not pay you overtime. That's why you hear about unions, where people organize."

"If I say I want more money, he will just give my hours to someone else."

"Sure, but it isn't right."

"It's not so bad."

"Where do you work?"

"Elegant Balloons."

It was a party supply place a few blocks away. It made for a strange villain, a balloon shop.

We reached her stop, and I told her I hoped she felt better.

THREE Mexican teenagers loaded in. They recognized the boy sitting across the aisle and greeted him. One of them asked if he still went to their church. He shook his head no.

"Who still goes there, now?" another wondered.

He shrugged.

"A bunch of little kids," he told them.

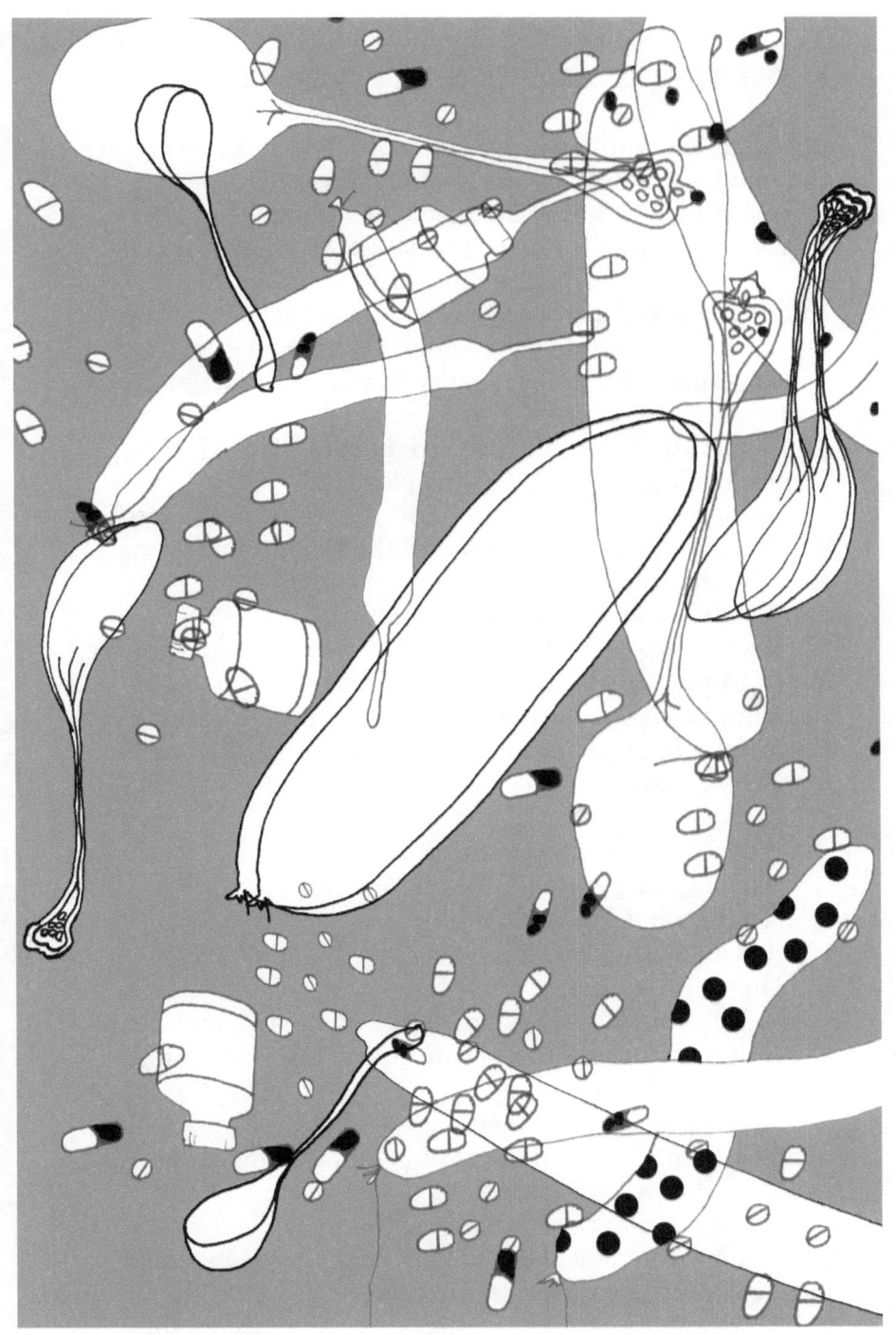

a hundred and twenty years

IT LOOKED like rain again, and I boarded the 217 North in
the middle of a friendly discussion between the female
driver and another middle-aged black woman in the
"conversation seat"—the one by the front doors, the only
place on the bus with an unobstructed view of the driver's
chair. The passenger wore a chocolate pleather trenchcoat
and a wig of straight brown hair. It was tousled the way
wigs inevitably are when they're put on in a hurry that
early in the morning.

"This rain is terrible," the driver said. "Everybody
slipping and sliding all over the place...."

"I heard the last big rain—not this week, but before—
four hundred people were killed," the woman in the wig
said. "Four hundred! That's a lot of people."

The driver shook her head.

"I see it every day," she said. "These people go running
out in front of traffic, or running after a bus. Too busy
thinking about something. They don't know. Whatever it is,
they would have plenty of time to think about it...waiting
for the next bus!"

"Okay?"

"People not paying attention...."

"People being *drunk*."

"That's what I'm saying!"

"People with *sexual* problems!"

They both laughed.

"...Running after they girl in the rain when she leaves
him," the woman in the wig continued. "All that rain...is
like an aphrodisiac!"

That broke them up again.

"We're bad, you and me both," she told the driver.

"It's all right sometimes."

The woman in the wig hoisted her heavy body with
some effort. She reached into her large purse, pulled out a
magazine, and handed it to the driver.

"Here you go, you have a nice day," she said as she

exited.

"Thank you, you do the same."

The driver glanced at the cover and put the magazine on the dashboard as passengers boarded. *Watchtower*.

"She gave me a Jehovah's Witness magazine," she said to no one in particular. "After all that."

VISIBLE through the window, a Korean teenager at the next stop sat waiting for another bus. The arrival of my bus barely registered; she remained absorbed in the Rubik's Cube she speedily manipulated using both hands. A large, hard-shell cello case rested against her knees. The lid was plastered with stickers that all looked printed by the same place. The largest was a big, square adhesive that read NATIONAL CELLO INSTITUTE...CELLO POWER! SINCE 1976. The rest were bumper stickers, simple black type on long white rectangles:

> I'M A FERMATA—HOLD ME
> GO HOME AND PRACTICE
> TUNE IT OR DIE
> GET OFF MY BACH
> I CAN'T, I HAVE REHEARSAL

And at the bottom, across the hips of the instrument:

> JESUS IS GOD. READ THE BIBLE.

CELIA was the older black woman I ran into occasionally, the drinker. She climbed the stairs of the bus haltingly as ever, but this time didn't appear to be tipsy. The thin brown leather of her thrift store bomber jacket was worn down to the lining in spots, and was unzipped enough to show off a second- or third-hand faded black T-shirt underneath. Peering out from her chest was an image of Cesare, the tragic sleepwalker from *The Cabinet of Dr. Caligari*. Probably she didn't know who he was, but I was pleased to see him anyway.

"How are you?" she asked, seating herself across from me. I nodded back.

"They said on television this is the most rain in a hundred and twenty years," she told me.

"That's a long time."

"It's a new record. A hundred and twenty years."

"At least we'll have a green spring," I said optimistically. "Lots of flowers."

"Yes, but it's the beginning of a circle. All this rain is gonna bring a whole lot of new greenery. And then all that greenery will dry out, and when it dries out, it'll start fires everywhere. Then the circle starts all over again." She gathered the purse in her lap up close and turned to stare out the front windshield. She shook her head.

"The big bad bear has to eat the poor little bunny. It's sad to think of it that way, but that's the way it is."

todos a lo largo de la atalaya

I WOKE up ten minutes ahead of the alarm. I'd had a surprisingly full night's sleep, considering the bad dreams that seemed to kick in from the moment my head hit the pillow.

They weren't like some nightmares, where you can almost enjoy them like a scary movie; or even like others, where the scope can be so vast and the terror so overwhelming, you can get swept up in the chaos of it all. Instead, these were small and intimate and dealt with the kinds of things you were too often forced to paint a smile on when faced with them in waking life. I got up, brushed my teeth, dressed and left for work.

AT THE bus stop, a small, butch woman in gray Dickies clamdiggers with tattoos on her neck (*mariposa*, one read) asked me if I had a quarter. Even short a quarter, they let you ride if you asked, but for some people pride got in the way. She was in her 40s, and politely desperate. I fished in my pockets for a coin. She was carrying an oversized box and her arms were full, but she half-opened a hand while keeping it clamped against one of the box's cardboard walls. I dropped the quarter into her palm where it clicked against the rest of her loose change. She got on the bus and was

still short the full fare, but the driver, a large black woman, waved her on, too deep in animated conversation on her cell phone headset to be bothered.

"What a day," the driver said. "It's true when they say it rains, it pours." It actually had been raining that morning. "Naw, they only paying $7.50 an hour. That's half of what I am making with MTA. Uh uh. Maybe that's what they pay *her*, but she's got no experience like I do…. No, my passenger told me that. Maybe. I don't know. They want to pay me nine dollars, I'll take it—but I'm putting nine dependents on that thing!"

She listened to the voice on the other end of the line a moment before interrupting it.

"You know me, I'm gonna do what I have to do."

Two sharply dressed black guys in their late 20s were by the back door.

"Damn!"

"What?"

"I forgot to get my backpack!"

"What backpack?"

"At American Eagle."

"American Eagle?"

"Yeah, last night. You spend thirty dollars or more, you're supposed to get a free backpack. I spent almost fifty!"

"Oh."

"Them shits come in handy! You can keep all kinds of stuff in there. Got someplace for your comb, a clean shirt, your smell-goods… Whatever you want."

"Yeah, your smell-goods…" his companion said absently.

"I forgot to ask for one, and they didn't give it to me."

WILLIAM drove the 842 over Laurel Canyon mornings. He was a trim, alert black man in glasses, his hair and neatly groomed moustache were going to snow, and he was never without a cap or cardigan. Yet despite a conservative appearance, he drove that little no-shocks-piece-of-crap shuttle bus harder and faster than anyone not blown out on PCP had surely ever dared to, and on a particularly winding and hazardous stretch of canyon road to boot. His early days introducing his white-knuckle driving style to the morning route were especially memorable. Commuters exchanged looks of strained amusement to hide the panic on their faces, and there were corners he rounded so sharply that even seated passengers clutched the handrails and set their teeth for disaster. But after a few months, either he eased up or they just got used to it. Maybe it was a little of both.

Lately the rain had been unusually severe, even for April. One heavily used section of Laurel Canyon had been declared too hazardous to travel and was partially closed down, with traffic re-routed down a parallel side street. But at 7:20 a.m. traffic was light, and nothing slowed William down very much anyway. As we approached the end of the line, I remarked that he got us there so fast there might as well not even have been a detour.

"That detour kept me over an hour yesterday," he said. "If I had done one more run, it would have been the straw that broke the camel's back."

"I bet," I told him. Coming home the opposite direction during rush hour, the traffic heading over the hill into the Valley was consistently bumper to bumper and immobile.

"You remember Laurel and Hardy?" he asked me.

"Sure."

"You remember when it would get to be too much, he would just..." He screwed up his face and clawed the air with his hands, making wheezing sounds through his nose.

"Oh yeah," I laughed.

"Well, that was because he had had the last straw."

"Right."

"He would go all to pieces. Hardy, not Laurel."

"Laurel would just cry."

"Yeah, he would just cry, or put his tie in his mouth or something."

AT THE Rapid stop, I was able to recognize the two sturdy brown girls from behind by their long, dark hair and big, round asses. They were there most days, though I had never been able to determine which of the four buses at the stop was theirs. They always wore ankle- or calf-length skirts, complemented by tight leather boots that started just below the knee. They were sexy in a natural, robust way, and to me they looked like office girls, the kind who leave the job when they get married, never to be heard from again. I had often thought about how they must stir the imaginations of their co-workers, whoever they were.

Unlike most mornings, they were joined by two others: a man and a woman, both older by at least ten years. He was small, in an off-the-rack olive suit and a Kangol cap. She was pasty and frail, and had done a patchy job shaving her legs. She seemed slightly ill at ease, as though she'd left the house without her knitting. As I got closer, I could see them by the bus bench, pointing out details in a magazine article to a middle-aged Guatemalan housekeeper seated there. It was *La Atalaya*, the Spanish-language version of the Jehovah's Witnesses' *Watchtower*. When a bus came and their prospect departed with it, they rejoined the two brown girls, regrouping in the shade of the Kinko's doorway near the other bus bench where I was sitting. There, the four of them staked out a fat, lonely-looking woman in sweatpants standing under the bus shelter across the street—until her bus arrived suddenly, and whisked her away unconverted.

The group broke and the two brown girls moved on to their next prospect at the Rapid stop, twenty feet away. I watched as they shared their literature and their message, realizing with disproportionate sadness that in all the weeks I'd been watching them, they'd never once thought me worth saving.

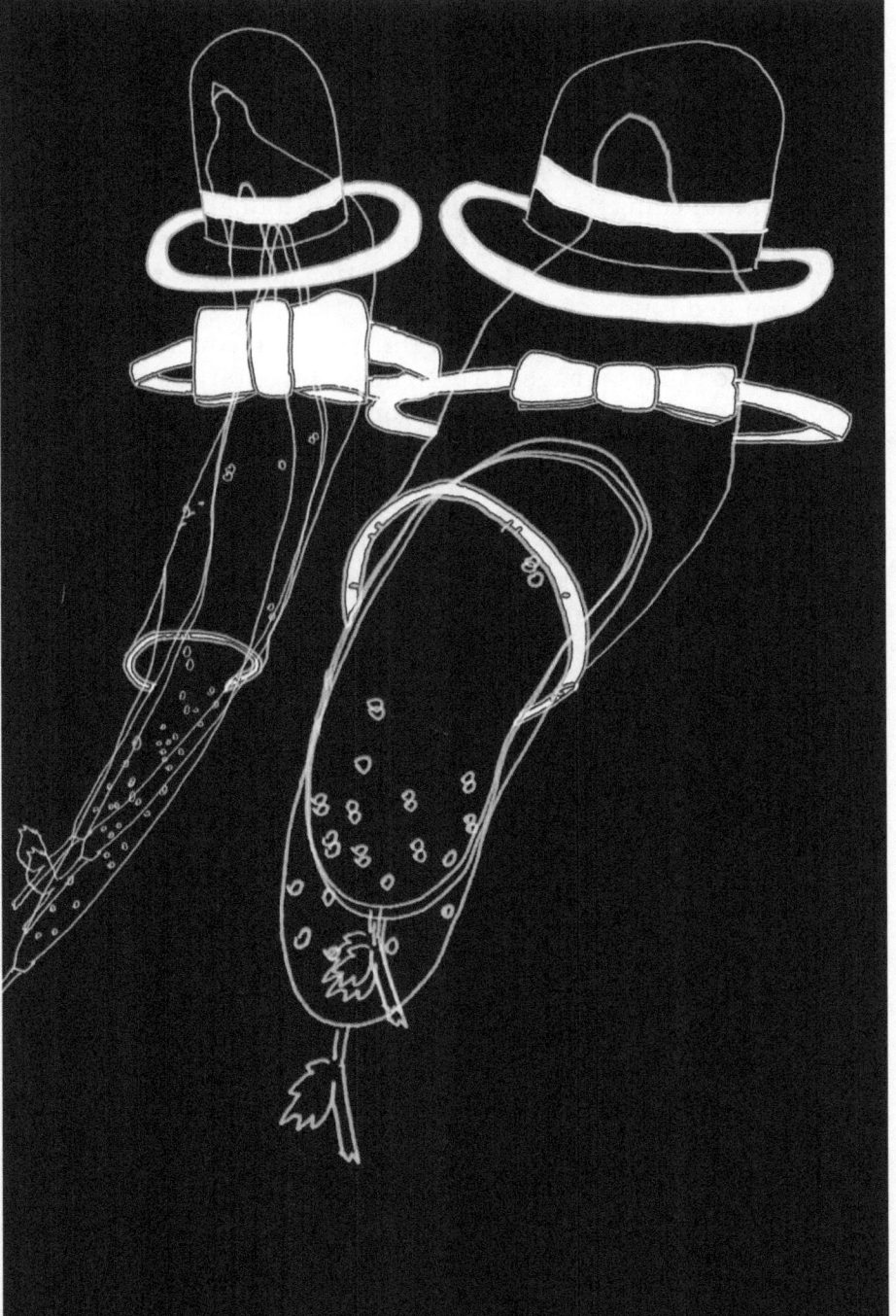

cowboy bebop

THE Red Line is a subway, but it's unusual to hear it called
one by anyone in Los Angeles who takes it. Maybe it's
because subways are something so many other cities have,
and in launching its own underground rail line, the MTA
was savvy enough to tap into the local compulsion to be
thought of as special; so in its promotion and to its riders,
it's the Red Line.

Universal City is a patch of real estate in North
Hollywood that manages to encompass an entertainment
conglomerate, a theme park, a shopping promenade and the
public transit hub across the street. Earlier that day, the
Red Line station there had been playing host to a film shoot
where it had been standing in for a sister station in Munich.
Posters on the walls promoting local destinations had been
temporarily covered by those advertising their Bavarian
cousins, and a pair of large, free-standing lightboxes
displayed clean, precise maps of the faraway city. A third
showcased a vibrant color portrait of Neuschwanstein, the
real-life fairytale castle.

In the station foyer, a round, guardhouse-style snack
stand—also part of the shoot—had been left unattended.
Its windows showcased exotic foreign chocolate bars and
dark-hued bottles of beer with necks wrapped in foil. But
these were only set dressing, amenities available to no one.
Not far off, a prop souvenir photo booth sat parked at an
inconvenient angle, its lighted exterior dim, its umbilical
power cord unplugged and splayed on the tile floor.

It all suggested a more sophisticated, civilized approach
to travel than any Los Angeles riders were accustomed to.
With a lone security guard all that remained of the film
crew for the moment, the set pieces were sure to be packed
away quickly as rush hour approached. Their ramshackle,
post-shoot placement was meant to ensure there'd be no
mistaking these props for actual services available to the
commuting public. They were merely tools of the trade the
city regularly stepped aside to facilitate, and no sign of
things to come.

CLIMBING aboard the bus that took me the rest of the way home, I took a seat in the last row, against the rear wall. One window was already occupied, and I chose the other. As the bus filled up, a black man in work denim sat between us.

Though the back row had the most seating of any on the bus, it was still unusual for someone to take a seat in the middle, at least when the adjacent side rows still remained open. It wasn't that it made for cramped seating so much as it tended to make people *feel* cramped; an almost legitimate grievance in a city notorious for its across-the-board sense of entitlement. My attention was out the window, watching the streets go by.

January can be cold even in Los Angeles, and for weeks the weather had been more severe than we were accustomed to. But the bus was humid with people, and I was warm in my heavy coat. The slat window above my head was open, and though the air inside was stale, when the bus moved the breeze felt refreshingly chilly.

A few minutes into the trip, my neighbor unfolded a big hooded sweatshirt and pulled it over his head. A fast-food takeout dinner in a wrinkled yellow plastic bag rested in his lap, and he tucked it under his sweatshirt to trap its warmth. His hands were weathered and rough, dirt under the nails.

"Did you want me to close this window?" I asked him.

"No, that's all right," he told me. "I was putting this on for when I get off, so I'll be warm."

His head was shaved, but a gray five o'clock shadow covered his cheeks and chin. He wore a thick, bushy moustache that drooped at the sides, like in old pictures of cowboys. Like them, his face had an honesty to it.

He chuckled a little. "This weather lately, you just never know. Sometimes it gets colder than you think it will. That's why I've always got one of these," he said, pulling out a knit watchman's cap to show me.

"I know what you mean," I said. "My room isn't heated, and there's been some nights where I'll wake up and can't get warm, even under blankets."

"It's been cold," he agreed, "real cold for out here. And it'll surprise you. You'll get on at one stop and by the time you get off at the other, the temperature will have dropped

even more. Then some days—like the other day—it'll be
fine. I'll tell you what, though: the last time the weather
was like this, with the Santa Ana winds blowing all their
stuff through and it was warm and then really cold? That
was right around the time of the Northridge earthquake.
Makes you wonder if that's what's coming, another big
earthquake."

"It definitely feels like its all building to something,"
I said. "But it's not just the weather. There's something
crazy in a lot of what's going on right now. Everything feels
knocked sideways."

"There's a lot of crazy things going on right now," he
agreed. "The weather, diseases, this war... Even with
people in general. Something's changed....

"People feel they don't even have to hear what you have
to say anymore, let alone try to win you over. Like talking
it out is a big waste of time, so now they're just gonna
steamroller on over you." He shook his head. "I didn't see
the speech on TV the other night, but I read it later. And I
don't get how you can talk about the state of the nation and
not even mention Katrina, and everything that still needs
to be handled down there. It's the greatest natural disaster
to hit this country in decades, and they're not even close to
where they should be, going on two years later."

"Everything I've seen about it says it could happen all
over again."

He nodded. "And it's not even just New Orleans—it's all
those states down there. It's Mississippi, Georgia, Alabama,
Florida...."

"Yeah, and to not talk about it in the State of the Union
address makes it seem like there's a reason for him not
talking about it, like it's a snub," I said. "Like, 'You've been
critical of me, so now I'm gonna treat you like it's a grade
school birthday party.' And if that's *not* the case, well, that
makes it even scarier."

"Things have changed for the good, too," he said. "We
have come a long way. Things are better in a lot of ways
than they used to be. In the past, there were a lot more
people went along with things they shouldn't have, that
they don't anymore. So it's definitely better than before.

"But this war in Iraq," he went on, "I don't get it.

When he first said he was declaring a 'war on terror,' I'll be honest, I thought he was through." He let out a hollow chuckle. "To have the President of the United States say something that makes as little sense as that and then put people's lives on the line.... I figured there's no way people would get behind that, let alone allow things to be where they are now. A 'war on terror'... I still can't find someone who can tell me what that even *means.*

"But people don't even talk about that anymore. You never hear anybody talking now about how a 'war on terror' is a meaningless idea from the beginning," he remarked. "See, once you've got American soldiers somewhere killing and dying every day, people can't even think about what started it. It's too much for people to get their heads around. All that death and killing ends up making a smokescreen—"

"The ultimate smokescreen," I added, pulling on the cord over the window to signal the driver the next stop was mine.

"...The ultimate smokescreen, for all the bullshit that was at the start of this whole thing! And now he wants to send more? Come on!

"I'll tell you this, though: when there's a war going on for no good reason, and somebody's telling you that you have to go and fight in it, there's a real simple solution: don't go! People just stick together and *don't go*! We did it before, and I was one of them. I was there."

The bus was coming to my stop. I stood and slung my bag over my shoulder. "Take care of yourself."

He smiled and nodded, then crooked his elbow and made a loose, friendly fist.

"One love," he said.

indestructionable

WILLIAM was driving the 842 over Laurel Canyon.

"So do you get a hour lunch or a half hour?" he asked me.

"I get an hour," I told him. "And one of the good things about my job is they have a cook on staff; they actually feed you."

"They feed you lunch?" He couldn't believe it.

"By the time I get in, she has breakfast ready, and then around noon she serves lunch."

"Do they really feed you, or they just give you a little something?"

"No, you can have as much as you like."

"So you can just pull your 'chuck up if you want," he laughed. "You ever been to the smorgasbord? I used to know this lady, she liked to go out to the smorgasbord. She loved the smorgasbord. You just don't see them anymore. You could bring your family, eat all day!"

"Sizzler still has that."

"Naw, Sizzler has a *salad bar*. A smorgasbord, you got chicken, potatoes…. There used to be one in Inglewood. I took that lady one time. She could throw down. She ate so fast, I said, 'If you eat any faster, you'll be *drinking* your food!' She liked to eat. She ended up going there so much, they had to shut the place down."

I stood up as we reached my stop.

"One day they just closed up the smorgasbord. 'OUT OF BUSINESS.'"

HE BOARDED the Woodman bus at Sherman Way, unevenly shifting his weight from foot to foot as he struggled to take each stair. His clothes were badly matched, and a plastic-sleeved photo ID emblazoned with a blue wheelchair icon dangled from a lantyard around his neck. In the picture, his head was tilted against the wall behind him, his eyes rolling back into his skull. His mouth gaped as if someone had just removed a fishhook.

He took a seat close to the front and sat in silence for a while before turning his attention out the window.

"I used to live in this neighborhood," he said to no one.

"It kind of went downhill pretty quickly."

He turned back around in his seat to face front.

"It's still a nice city."

THE DRIVER of my next bus wasn't a tall woman, and she had cranked her seat up to sit a little higher behind the wheel.

"What are you doing all the way up there?" Celia wondered, laughing as she boarded. Celia was the older black woman who often turned up tipsy at that hour of the morning. She was wearing a loose sweatshirt and baggy jeans, topped with a red knit ski hat and joined us a few stops ahead of her usual.

"Good morning," she said, taking a seat directly across from me. "Can I ask you something? What do people think happens when you mix oil and water? Because these people drive like it's no big deal. Like you ain't gonna *slide!*"

It hadn't rained for days, but the last time it had must have stayed with her. She raised the pitch of her voice in imitation of a spoiled child.

"They think, 'It's just a little rain. I live in *California*, nothing's gonna happen to me.' People think they're indestruction..." She considered the word before correcting herself. "...*Indestructionable.*

"Driver," she called out, "Can I ask you a question? How is it that it's my grandson's birthday, and he's thirteen and I'm only thirty-three?" She let out a short blast of a cackle and stood up.

"You have a nice day," she told me, and moved down the stairs with a wobbly uncertainty, as if acclimating to gravity.

When she reached the curb, she stopped and surveyed her surroundings with some suspicion, unwittingly blocking at every turn a small elderly Asian woman's attempts to board the bus. With impeccable timing and painful inevitability, Celia would look one way as the Asian woman tried to pass her on the other. And the moment the Asian woman patiently moved out from the blind spot, Celia returned to it. It was a *pas de deux* they repeated several times in a silent comedy so exasperating it couldn't have been choreographed any more tragically. The Asian woman looked pleadingly to the driver, desperate to not be left behind.

Finally Celia, still oblivious, slowly turned to look back up into the bus.

"Driver, I'm sorry. I wanted Magnolia."

polkadots and moonbeams

"DID you look up that Dexter Gordon record I told you about, *One Flight Up*?"

William was pushing the 842 hard up Laurel Canyon, and the small bus rattled with the effort. I could barely hear him over the racket and had to ask him to repeat himself.

"*One Flight Up*. The record I told you about yesterday," he said.

"Yeah, yeah. I might try to pick that up this weekend."

"It's out of print, isn't it?"

"No, you can get it on CD."

"You can? Well that was one of Dexter Gordon's most popular records! You know it only has three tracks on it. 'Tanya' takes up the whole first side, then the other side is 'Coppin' The Haven,' then a ballad, 'Darn That Dream.'"

"I know 'Darn That Dream'. Not his version, but I know the song."

"You do?" he asked, singing at full voice:

> *Darn that dream*
> *I dream each night*
> *You say you love me*
> *and hold me tight...*

I was impressed, as you are when your bus driver breaks into song with such gusto, while he drives a crowded bus through traffic up a crooked road at 7:30 in the morning.

"That's a standard," he told me as he finished.

"Right," I said. "Hey, when you used to play, did you ever use a fake book?" Fake books, bootleg sheet music collections; they've probably saved more working musicians than the Bible.

"Sure, but you know, some of them would have different changes. You can lose the whole song if you don't have the right changes. You don't have the right changes, you're lost right from jump street. You have to know the inside before you can go outside. Otherwise, you go outside and you're in no-man's land! Do you know that tune, 'Polkadots and Moonbeams'?"

"Yup."

"That was the first song I learned to play. I took lessons from a guy, ten dollars a lesson, once a week."

"Ten dollars sounds expensive. For then, I mean."

"*Then* it was. Now...."

"Now, it's nothing."

"Now, it's nothing. But I wanted to go a couple times a week! He said no, you can't force it. He would send me off with enough to work on for the whole week. I would practice six, eight hours a day.

"I saw him again, years later. Maybe '73, '75. I was in the drugstore, in line to get a prescription filled, and I recognized him right away. I said, 'Do you know me?' And he looked at me and said, 'Give me a minute, your face looks familiar.'" He laughed at the memory. "He always had a lot of students. He still teaches piano."

"He's still around?" I asked, surprised.

"Yeah!" he said defensively. "He's only a few years older than I am! He was the one who told me, 'Music is not a hobby. It's a way of life.' He was right. You'd see all these guys, and they were good players! But they were poor.

"I studied with him that way for four years, but then I started thinking, I want things. I want a house, you know? They saw me coming around in like, a Cadillac, and they were saying, 'You have to give up these material things!'

"But I saw the ramifications of the lifestyle, and I said this is not for me. I don't regret my decision. I knew that's not what I wanted—living in a house with a bunch of musicians, none of them having a pot to piss in."

It was unusual to hear someone talk about a dream they'd left behind without even a twinge of regret or sadness, but he meant what he said.

"I watched a show on TV last night, *America's Most Talented Teens*? This kid was on playing saxophone. You know Herbie Hancock's 'Cantaloupe Island'? He played

that. He soloed on it and everything. He had a alto. And he could play! He was up against a tap dancer and two singers."

"How'd he do?" I asked.

"Well, the judges are kids, too; so they don't really know. I mean, I feel like anyone can sing as long as they have a good voice to start with."

"Right."

"But naw, those judges didn't give him anything. The tap dancer won."

two playboys

IT WAS late, and I was alone on the bus until he boarded and took the seat across the aisle. Settling in, he reached into his hip pocket and took out a glossy, digest-sized giveaway guide to the local strip clubs.

Thumbing through, he paused to linger on a two-page spread, a tacky series of shots documenting the contortions of an especially limber entertainer as she folded herself up like a mash note on the floor of an anonymous black stage.

Catching a glimpse of me over his shoulder, he held the booklet up where he was sure I could see it, pushed out his pale tongue, then buried his face in the pictures and excitedly pretended to lick the pages, delighting in his own shamelessness.

He could see, but his vision was poor and he squinted the way some blind people do. It took some getting used to. And though without a tooth in his head, he somehow resembled Al Jarreau, right down to the singer's trademark ebullience. So, a toothless Al Jarreau, blind but ebullient, on the bus, licking pictures of strippers.

He turned another page, stopping on a picture of a chesty blonde overflowing her bikini top; it was an ad for a topless place located in a nearby industrial park. He gently traced the outline of her mammoth breasts with his finger.

"That's what I like!" he announced in a deep, froggy voice. Then qualified it: "But I like 'em when they're real."

"Good luck with that at a strip club," I offered.

"I ain't ever even been to a strip club!"

"No?"

"Nope. I know I couldn't go. Because if I did, I'd have to leave and go home. Looking wouldn't be enough!" He turned a few more pages, surveying the catalogue. "White women, black women... Everybody's okay with me. Lord God made all of us!"

He furrowed his brow, thinking hard. "What's the name of the place, it's like a farmers market, people buy food there? That's where I came from before. I saw so many beautiful women there! Women as beautiful as this." He pointed to the porn star on the cover.

"I asked one lady, 'Is this Heaven? Have I died and gone to Heaven? Because this is what it must be like!'

"This lady, she was so beautiful. I went up and I told her, 'A man could wait his whole life to be with a woman as beautiful as you. His whole life!' Her face got so flushed. She loved to hear that!"

He continued browsing the pictures before selecting a full-page ad of a stripper in a thong to present to me. The model was bent at the waist, and the photograph's foreshortening enlarged her round ass to cartoonish effect.

"Look at that!" he hooted, petting the image. "I have a girlfriend, but she's not like this!" He closed the guide as if it had become too much for him and turned in his seat to better face me. "I had a girl—Yolanda—she had those great big calves and thick, solid thighs... Whoo!" he shook his head.

"What happened to her?"

"I don't know what happened to her," he said, genuinely uncertain. He thought a moment. "I was on medication then, so I couldn't even fuck her. All I could do was lick her pussy and kiss her titties. She would say, 'Now I know that's not *all* you're gonna do!' Ha ha ha! I wish I could find her again. I'm not on that medication anymore. Nowadays, I get hard when the *wind* blows!"

He resumed his admiration of the woman in the ad. "I've never paid for sex before. I never had to. But if it was a girl like that? I would pay. I would pay $500 to have sex with her all night. But," he insisted, "it would be *all night*! I would tell her I was going to fuck her until she was coming out of her *ears*! I would say to her, 'When I leave in the morning, I want to be *drained!*'" He was extremely pleased at the notion.

"I think I'd like to be in X-rated movies," he said. "That's the job for me!"

"You think so?"

"I've never had any complaints," he said philosophically.

He was so sincerely tickled at his own capacity for lasciviousness, it was hard to be offended. And anyway, it was just me, him and the driver on an otherwise empty bus.

We got out at Hollywood and Highland.

"I need to go to La Brea," he said, "to catch the 212. I can get the 217 and get off at La Brea, or I can walk from here to the bus stop there."

"You know you can catch the 212 here, too," I said.

"You can? I didn't even know that! That's perfect. Say, do you smoke cigarettes?" he asked.

"No, I don't, sorry."

"That's okay! I just bought a pack of Marlboros; you could have one if you smoked." I'd been hit up for cigarettes by strangers at bus stops most of my life, but I'd never before been offered one.

He pulled the pack from his pocket and stuck one into his lips, splitting a seam at the filter. He held the flame to it, but the air kept escaping through the tear and the light wouldn't take. He didn't seem to notice, and kept working at it.

"So what do you do with your days?" I asked him as we strolled together to the stop.

"Well, today I went to see my attorney, about my lawsuit. It's a million dollar lawsuit. I agreed he gets one-third. I think one-third of a million is three hundred thousand dollars?"

"Close enough to it."

"Kleinman and Morris. It's a famous law firm. Have you heard of it?"

"No, but I don't really know law firms."

"Kleinman and Morris. My lawyer's in charge, he has a bunch of other lawyers work for him. It's a whole office full of lawyers, and I get the boss!" He considered it a minute. "You know about Jewish people, right? That's how I know he's going to work hard to help me. Because then he'll get three hundred thousand dollars!"

"Nobody doesn't like getting paid," I said.

"That's right! He'll get that, and I'll get what's left over."

"What's your lawsuit over?"

"You know where Hollywood Boulevard and Western is? Down there?" he pointed. "That's where it happened. It was on Hollywood Boulevard at Western. I was hit by a _____." It was a noisy night and his missing teeth made the word completely unintelligible.

"I'm sorry," I said. "You were hit by a what?"

"A *ambalence*," he repeated.

"You were hit by an ambulance?"

He nodded. "My lawyer says I was lucky; because I'm a forty-six-year-old man, I didn't have to be wearing a bicycle helmet. If I had been eighteen or under, it would have been against the law to not have one on. I wouldn't have a case."

"So was it racing off somewhere?"

"No, she just wasn't paying attention, because she was talking on her cell phone. Six people saw her and wrote down the license plate number."

"She hit-and-runned you?"

"She hit-and-runned me. I don't think she knew she even hit me!"

"What happened?"

"I was riding my mountain bike along on Hollywood"—I tried to picture him riding a mountain bike down busy Hollywood Boulevard—"I was going to get up on the sidewalk, and she came around the corner and hit me. I spun around a bunch of times and cracked my head on the concrete. My head was split right open."

"Man!" I said, picturing the scene. "Well, at least people saw it. And they all took down the license plate? That's six angels, right there."

"Yes," he agreed. "God was with me."

He bent forward, blinking at the traffic. "Look at that!" he cried, squinting at a beautifully maintained Charger paused at the light.

"When I win my lawsuit, I want to get a 2007 Bentley. But I like those cars, too! Muscle cars. Those old Chargers, or a Camaro, or a Chrysler Columbus... I know a lot about cars. You know the Lamborghini, the new Lamborghini, has a jet engine in it?"

"A jet engine?" I asked skeptically.

"Oh, maybe not a jet engine, not the same size as the planes have. Those are really big."

"Maybe they say it works the same way?"

"Maybe that's what it is."

He surveyed the trendy clothing retailers in the mall behind us. "You know, these stores around here, they're expensive. You go shopping in them, and pretty soon you won't have any money left! That's not where my money's gonna go. I'll invest in property!"

"Sounds like a smart way to go."

"I'll go to government auctions, buy a property there. Then fix it up myself! You know how Mexicans are real good with carpentry? What I'll do is hire a bunch of Mexicans to fix it up with me. And I'll take real good care of them! I'll pay 'em good, and have good lunches for everybody. I'll buy them cigarettes. I'll say, 'What kind of cigarettes do you like to smoke? Marlboros? Camels?' I'd treat them like they were my own brothers! Because you have to treat people the way you want to be treated."

He suddenly noticed an average-looking girl with mocha skin a few feet away. Without hesitating, he broke from me to approach her.

"Hey girl," he said. "You really got it going on, you know that? What's your name?"

She ignored him.

He tried to adopt a casual attitude, staying near her and reclining against the post that displayed the buses' timetable. But the pole was far too thin for leaning, and he slipped off at the shoulder; he had to catch himself to keep from falling. Recovering, he walked back to my side.

"She knows she's fine," he told me. "She's probably got a man she's going home to, that's why she won't give me any action." He was very understanding about it.

"You gotta try," he told me. "You see a pretty girl, you gotta talk to her. Women like to talk to me. They'll flirt with me and play, but then you want to say, 'Let's go home and get out of these clothes.' Hey, it's got to work sometime!"

"It's a numbers game," I offered.

"Ha! You're a playboy, too! I can tell! You probably got some good pussy waiting on you right now!" His dim eyesight hampered his sense of personal space, and each time he spoke he moved in closer.

"I have never been with a white woman," he continued, "but I would like to! I think all women are beautiful, I don't care what color they are.

"Sometime, I want to go to the clubs, like the clubs here on Hollywood Boulevard. When I win my lawsuit, I'll get all dressed up in nice clothes and go to the clubs and meet some of those big, beautiful white women. Mexican women, black women..."

His eyes didn't need to be open for me to recognize a faraway look in them.

"That's the 217 coming now," I said, looking down the street. "You gonna take that to La Brea or wait here for the 212?"

"I'll get on and ride to La Brea with you," he said.

It was only about three blocks. There weren't many seats open, but we found two by the back door. The evening buses always felt dirtier at the end of the workday, and this one smelled of stale foreign takeout and homelessness.

"You smell that?" he asked me, putting his nose in the air. A few seats down and across the aisle, a fat, noticeably unshowered white man wearing several layers of clothes glowered over his shoulder, awaiting an insult.

"Somebody," my companion sniffed, not even noticing the other man. "...Smells *good* on this bus!" He took a deep breath, analyzing it. "That's Eternity, by Calvin Klein. Somebody's wearing Eternity. I like that!"

La Brea came up quickly, and he rose to go. He offered me a handshake.

"It was nice to meet you," he said. "Maybe I'll see you again sometime.... And if I do, we'll go to a strip club!"

He leaned in, squinty eyes squeezed shut, still holding my hand. "Don't worry," he assured me, lowering his voice. "I'll treat you."

Probably he winked.

bringing up daisy

MY EARS popped, which meant we had reached the peak of
Laurel Canyon and were about to descend into the Valley.
William was driving the 842, and we were running a few
minutes late.

"Did you ever hear about the guy—I forget his name—
he was The Jazz Whistler?" he asked me.

"A jazz whistler?"

"Yeah. He was bad." Meaning good.

"All he did was whistle?"

"Yeah, he was The Jazz Whistler!"

"But he didn't start out as something else and also
whistle?"

"Naw, he had a band behind him, and he would stand
down front and whistle. But he could play! He was in tune,
he would do runs and things.... You never heard of him?"

"I definitely never heard of him."

"Hm. I was thinking about him the other day. My friend
was telling me about how, to get in the NBA, you have to be
able to do one thing. You got to focus on only one thing, like
rebounds. Or maybe you're a shooter. But you perfect one
thing... You get to be the best at one thing, and you're in
there."

"You saying I gotta get practicing my whistle?" I asked.

He shrugged.

"Well, maybe you ain't a whistler."

I DON'T wear a watch, so when the woman asked me what
time it was, I pointed to the flashing LED sign at the
front of the bus that scrolled out the date and time at
regular intervals. She nodded and shook her head, a little
embarrassed she hadn't thought of that herself. 7:25, it
read, and I relayed it to her. I didn't mind. She was an older
lady, and seeing the thick lenses in her glasses, I figured
she could use the help.

I returned to my book—a rock drummer's memoirs—but
she caught my attention before I could retreat back into it.

"What are you reading?" she asked me. Her gravelly

diction made me think she may have been deaf and lip-reading.

I held it up.

"It's an autobiography."

She didn't recognize it.

"He's a musician," I explained.

"Is it good?" she asked.

"It's okay."

She smiled politely.

"I got it for twenty-five cents." It seemed relevant to let her know I was ready to cut some slack to something that cost so little.

She rummaged through her bag and pulled out a battered old paperback. Barely held together by dried, crumbling masking tape and a rubber band wrapped around its middle, she held it out to show me. The cover was a photograph in comforting, saturated 1950s color: a woman reaching up to stroke the neck of a giraffe. The title was *Bringing Up Daisy*, and it purported to be a true story.

"How is it?" I asked.

"I like animals," she said, almost apologetically.

farther than rome

THERE had been an accident at Ventura and Woodman
shortly before I arrived. Broken pieces of taillight plastic
scattered the asphalt, crunched and dragged by passing
traffic. A damaged vehicle had pulled off into the parking
lot of the furniture store on the corner.

Its four passengers had escaped unharmed, and all
spoke into cell phones in varying degrees of intensity. I
overheard one say "hit and run" as I walked the few feet to
the bus stop, where I waited.

The gaggle of matronly Latina domestics who rode the
bus were all there as usual, chattering about the collision
some of them had witnessed minutes earlier. Standing
apart from them, a balding Armenian in his 30s, sporting
sunglasses and a leather Members Only jacket. A plastic
grocery bag hung heavily from one hand, and a dozen white
roses wrapped in cellophane lay cradled in his other arm.

As the bus pulled around, the small Mexican lady
who got off near the mall came over to say hello. She
was easygoing, and loved chit-chat. She had a warm
and familiar way about her that made you feel almost
comforted. From our weeks of small talk, I knew she had
daughters, and she'd be a dream grandmother.

Boarding, the Armenian sat next to her and across
from me. I was rummaging through loose papers in my
bag when she called to get my attention. I looked up to see
the Armenian smiling broadly, his hand hanging in the air
expectantly, waiting for me to complete a hi-five. I reached
up and lightly smacked his palm, wondering if I knew him
from somewhere or if he was just crazy; after a minute, I
realized I didn't know him.

"What happened back there?" the grandmother asked me.

"An accident," I told her. "I didn't see it."

She asked the Armenian if he had, and he responded in
an accented voice.

"The Hispanic guy fell down, and then they held him
down and he died."

"What?!" she cried, aghast.

"They killed him," he said simply. "They killed him because he was a nice guy."

"Who?" she asked him.

"Those guys," he said. He pointed out the front windshield, where there was nothing to see but the street ahead disappearing beneath us as we drove.

"He was in the holding cell, and he wanted to go home, and he fell. They held him down and killed him. In front of me and this other guy."

"Oh, I see," she said. She looked at me.

"Were you there for the car accident?" I asked him.

"Hey, I don't care about the cars, buddy," he stated simply, offering a pleasant smile.

"What is your family's nationality?" she asked him, changing the subject.

"Armenian."

"My boss is from your country," she told him. "But he was born in New York. He's a very nice person."

"I like him, too," he said agreeably. He took out a can of Chef Boyardee from the plastic bag he was carrying and showed it to her.

"Spaghetti," she said.

"Ooh, *si señora*. Spaghetti is very famous. I ate a whole big plate of it before," he said. "Would you like a rose?"

"Sure," she said.

He pulled a white rose from the bunch and handed it to her. He asked the ladies seated behind her if they would also like roses. They all did, and they giggled like schoolgirls as he presented the flowers to them.

"Is this for Mother's Day?" one of them asked.

He appeared confused, so the lovable grandmother rephrased it for him with less of a question in her voice.

"These are for Mother's Day," she said, as though confirming it. He shrugged and agreed they were.

He looked at me. "Do you want one?"

The ladies tittered. But his offer was sincere, so I smiled and took it in that spirit—though I declined the flower.

"Are you happy?" he asked me. He turned to the women. "He is such a handsome guy," he said, and they giggled again.

"This is number one best flower," he assured them. "I

don't like red rose."

Another housekeeper boarded, and as she dug for her pass, he handed her a rose.

"Oh! Thank you!" she said, pleasantly surprised.

He pulled another from the bunch and handed it to her.

"That one is for her," he said, indicating the bus driver.

"That's very sweet," the driver said.

"I have to save at least one for my girlfriend," he explained, "or she will be mad at me."

At their stop, the group of ladies got up to leave.

"Thank you for the flowers," they chorused unevenly, still giggling girlishly. His face lit up, pleased to find himself on the receiving end of so much easy goodwill.

He looked at me and reached into his bag to show me the can of pasta. He pointed to the picture on the front.

"We can take these out," he said, indicating the meatballs, "and it will be good."

"Sure."

"You know where you can get the best spaghetti? Domingo's," he said, slurring a little.

"Domino's?"

"*Domingo's.* It's on Ventura Boulevard. You know how much a plate of spaghetti costs you?"

"How much?"

"Free," he said triumphantly. "Ask for Tony. Tell him Jerry told you. He'll give you a big plate of spaghetti— free. You try to give him money and he'll knock you out, probably.

"You know where I am from?" he asked me. He reached into his inside jacket pocket and drew out a half-empty quart bottle of Heineken. He performed an exaggerated double take at the sight of it, then replaced it inside his coat. From his other pocket he pulled out a pack of cigarettes decorated with exotic lettering and an illustration of an ancient columned temple.

"This is where I am from," he said, holding the cigarettes out.

"Where is that?"

"Farther than Rome," he said solemnly. "I am not lying."

He put the cigarettes away and took out the beer again, drinking much of what was left in a long swallow. As he did, I noticed a plastic band on his wrist with his name printed on it. It was the kind of identification they give you in county facilities; a jail, or a hospital.

Leaving a small amount in the bottle, he tucked it away in his jacket. He leaned back in his seat, his fingers searching blindly behind him for the cord to signal his stop. It took him a few tries to catch the wire that rang the bell. As the bus slowed to a halt, he stood to go.

"Take care," I told him. He turned around as if he'd forgotten something and came back to me, holding up a hand. We hi-fived goodbye.

From our seats, the driver and I watched him stumble off to wherever it was he was headed.

"That could have gone a bunch of ways," I told her.

"Yes, it could have," she agreed. "But he was peaceful."

last of the mohicans

"You know Sonny Rollins?"

"Sure."

"You know about him?"

"Not too much."

"Well, all through the '50s he had a pretty successful career going, but something inside was telling him he should give up all those good gigs and go play on his own, out in public; that he should go play on the bridge. So that's what he did. He went out and played on the bridge. He was on that bridge for three years! Then he returned to performing as a professional, and you know what his first record was when he came back?"

"What?"

"*The Bridge.*"

An old man was sitting in my usual seat, so I waited a few stops until the one across from him opened up, and I moved into it.

He was thin and bald, and in his blue zippered cardigan and trousers he looked like an elderly postal clerk, weary

from decades of dealing with humanity at its most petty
and hostile. He had birdlike features, but up close what was
most striking was the unusual texture of his skin; it gave
him the appearance of a yellowing wax figure.

His fingers held a bus pass labeled SENIOR pinched to a
small piece of thin gray cardboard, the back of a scratchpad.
There he'd carefully and precisely laid out his route away
from and back to the Valley in neat block capitals.

I lost track of him when I changed buses at Ventura,
but it turned out we were going the same way. Somehow
he even managed to beat me to the Woodman stop; he was
already waiting on the bench when I emerged from my bus.
When the 158 arrived, I let him board ahead of me out of
courtesy, and goddamned if he didn't take my usual seat on
that bus, too.

"So WHEN Sonny came back, that's when he'd shaved his
head?"

"He shaved his head into a *Mohican*. You would see
them sometimes. You still see them. I had a kid in my class
when I was at school come in with a Mohican one time.
That didn't really go over. The teachers..."

"They didn't like that?"

"Naw, they made him wear... Have you ever heard of
ringwart, where you get the things in your hair and you
have to shave your head? When you would get that, there's
these little white hats they would make you wear, they
covered your head and tied around your chin with a string."

"Like a bonnet?"

"Yeah! It was like a bonnet. They made him wear one
of those, to cover up his Mohican. Kids would tease the hell
out of him."

"I bet. So they made him wear that to shame him? So he
would want to get in step with everybody else?"

"Well, the other kids were all very interested in his
Mohican. It was getting to be a distraction."

HIGH school is where there's the most talk about peer
pressure, but the battle's fought and lost earlier than
that. It happens in grade school, particularly in Catholic
schools like I went to. Built into all the instruction in good

manners and social niceties was a kind of blind obedience
to authority, a real "take it and like it" attitude that no
one ever really pushed back against, or at least didn't push
very hard. Not that there weren't "bad kids"—every class
had those—but misbehavior is different from opposition
on anything like what you might later call philosophical
grounds.

Probably the closest I saw to pushing back was
Jim Scott, in seventh grade. Jim was a quiet kid, never at
the top of the class. At school, he was easy to get along with
and well-liked. He was a handsome kid, and good-hearted.

He lived with his mom and two sisters, giving him a
"man of the house" status that I think I must have found
enviable at the time. Eight years of school with the same
class of thirty-odd kids, you got to know each other pretty
well—or at least as well as you know anyone at that age.
Besides that, we were both tall, and that meant we were
regularly partnered off in line. Our mothers knew each
other and we were friends.

The year before, in sixth grade, we'd somehow been
lucky and landed Mrs. Meehan as a teacher. She was
new to the school and one of the few teachers there who
genuinely liked working with kids; naturally we all
adored her. Then a year later, the poles shifted and we
were handed over to a nun called Sister Joan, who had
about as vicious and vindictive a personality as any we'd
encountered up to that point.

Encouragement in Sister Joan's classroom was
nonexistent. Mrs. Meehan had been able to make us feel
that we were part of her life and meant something to her;
nice at any age, but especially meaningful then. It brought
out the best in us. We never learned anything about
Sister Joan except that she couldn't fucking stand us. "God
says I must love you, but I don't have to *like* any of you,"
she'd often remind us, managing to lawyer her way around
The Almighty's Own Message of Love to shit on us. We were
treated as though we had a lot to answer for, and mostly
what I remember is her tearing into us day after day with
name-calling, snide remarks and constant references to the
shame we brought on our parents.

The way she'd bring our folks into it was a particularly

cheap shot, and she'd insulate herself from blowback by telling you exactly what she was sure they *musn't* be. In short, you *had* to be the kind of shit-eater who brought naught but shame on your parents, since surely you didn't come from a whole *family* of shit-eaters? These were your choices. You wouldn't take it from any knucklehead in the schoolyard, but this was the teacher. And if you wanted to be a Good Kid, you didn't have much choice. You had to get used to keeping your hands folded and your mouth shut.

Looking back, the level of hostility she showed us was outrageous, but at the time we accepted it as simply the way things were. We didn't know any better.

Who could figure out what she was always barking about? After a point, it didn't seem to matter very much to her or to us; but every day it was something. She would swing, and we would duck. Sometimes she missed, sometimes she connected; we kept our hands at our sides either way.

What brought on her picking on Jim that particular day I can't remember. Probably he was called on to read aloud and she felt he was mumbling (he was a lousy reader, and it embarrassed him), or maybe it was over a question he just didn't know the answer to; it wouldn't have been the first time for either. She opened up on him for a bit while the rest of the class squirmed in their desks, then she decided to up the ante.

"Stand up, James," she told him. "Are you an idiot, James? Are you a dummy? Are you a little baby? Should I get you a pacifier?"

"No," he answered quietly.

"What did you say? I can't hear you, little baby."

"No."

"Pardon me?"

"No, Sister."

"*Mwm mwam?*" she asked, in gross exaggeration of his soft-spoken discomfort. That kind of low-blow teasing was a familiar technique, deployed on anyone who dared show discomfort while being humiliated in front of everyone they knew. It was doubly effective in that it not only embarrassed the victim, but encouraged nervous classmates to laugh at them as well; the more the merrier.

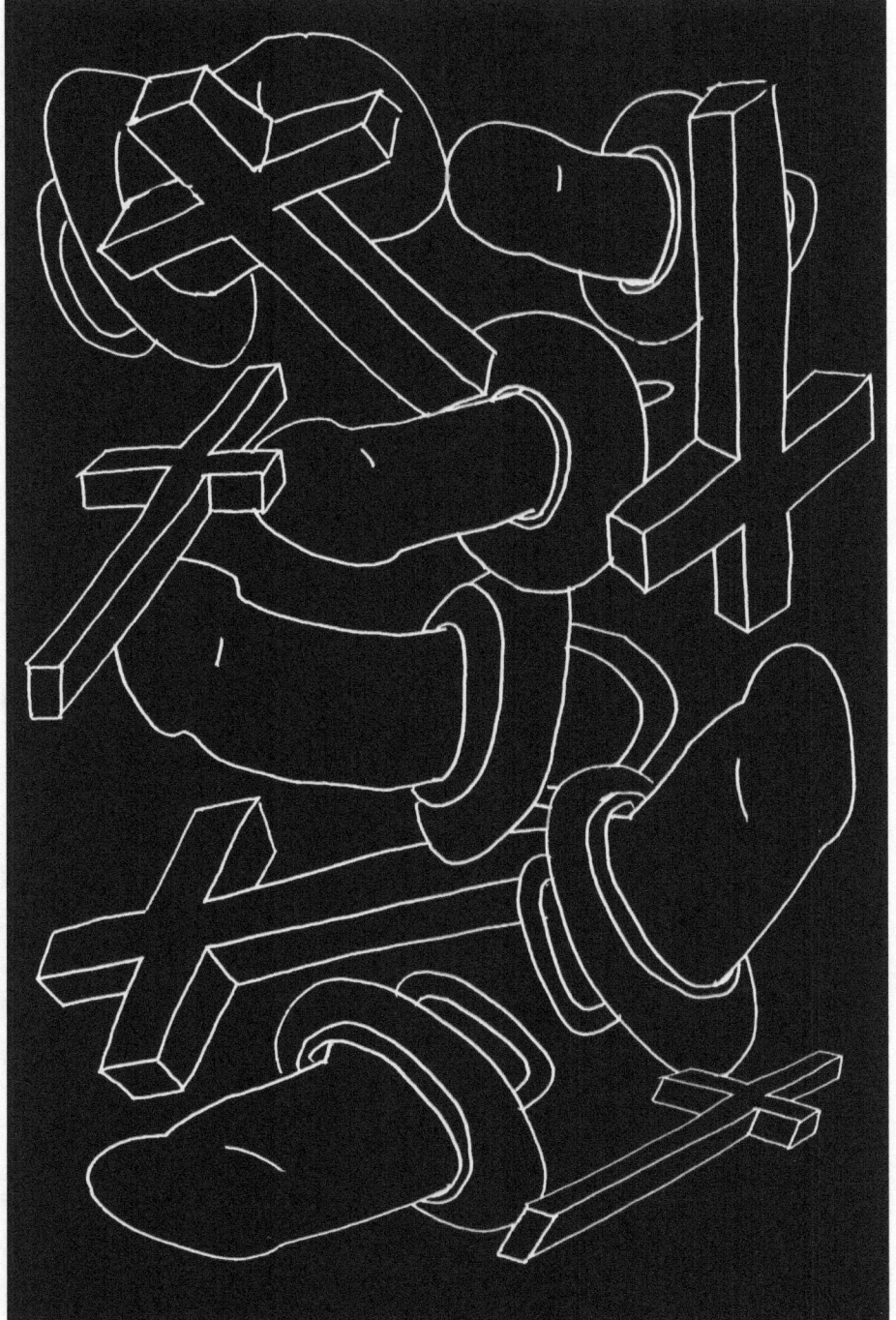

That was the thing about her, and so many of the teachers I grew up with: there was never any such thing as a simple mistake. Every misstep was a brazen affront to be countered with swift discipline, discipline that inevitably took the form of public disgrace.

"Well," she said, "if you're going to be a dummy, then you can stand there like a dummy." She left him standing alone next to his desk while she returned to the blackboard to resume the lesson.

My desk was near Jim's, and as the minutes passed, I could see him tense up and tremble a little as he struggled unsuccessfully to fight back tears. Then something inside him suddenly rose up and took over. Picking up his books, he walked to the back of the room to the coat closet, where he collected his jacket and bookbag before starting down the row to the front of the classroom. It took Sister Joan a moment to pick up on the murmurs and turn around to see for herself what was happening.

"Excuse me, sir," she said, using formal address with thick sarcasm, as she often did.

He ignored her.

"*Excuse me, sir*," she called out to him.

He kept on going, straight to the door.

"Do not open that door, sir! *Do not open that door!*"

But he did open it. He opened it, and he walked through, and he never said a word in reply. For once, she had no idea what to do, no clue how to respond to this little mutiny. Her features locked in a flat, smug smile, a look of constipated scorn that was her most familiar expression. A moment—under the circumstances, an eternity—passed before finally she sniffed contemptuously, as if she had somehow trumped *him*, and resumed writing on the blackboard. I prayed—I really did!—that the low orthopedic heel would break off her shoe, that her chalk would snap as a final indignity, as a perfect punctuation mark to the event. But nothing happened.

My seat was close to the window, and with Sister Joan's back to the class, I was able to see Jim exit the building, walk down the schoolyard driveway and off school grounds. He never turned to look back. Probably it didn't even occur to him to.

I was a kid, and though I couldn't have explained it,

I was still able to recognize he'd done something potent, something significant. It wasn't grandstanding. It wasn't telling her to shove it, or even firing back and calling her names, as she had done to him. While she trotted out petty humiliations and put on mocking voices, he responded to her taunts the way any reasonable person might: he simply left.

And in that environment, where sucking it up and choking it down was quietly accepted as the cost of doing business, simply pushing away from the table and walking out the door became something kind of noble.

el designado

TWO shopping carts sat parked in the alcove between storefronts on Ventura, both filled to capacity with street detritus wrapped in plastic bags of varying sizes. Most mornings that's where the two Mormon girl recruiters strategized conversions and gossiped the Good News, but today they were nowhere to be seen. In their place was Nutter Butter, a thin black street madman, loudly holding court in stained jeans and filthy Fightin' Irish baseball cap.

"You on *parole*," he growled as I made my way to the bus stop. The inside of his mouth was chalky and swollen, looking like chewed dough behind his broken teeth.

He had a heavy accent from somewhere in Dixie, and his voice was loud and rooster-shrill. He had the rhythm and cadence of a livestock auctioneer; he was born to yell.

"Keep on walking! Don't even *think* about stopping, or I'll kick your *ass*. You on *parole*." Chin to his chest, he rolled the last word while his eyes, hooded and intense, followed me as I passed.

"You can't be showin' up on me like we all good like that, like I'm your *butler*!" He tossed his head. "Don't try that shit on me!"

Moving out of his line of vision didn't calm him or stop his yelling, but that was okay. His fiery rant was pure rage, invective and sheer, fearless crazy. In its strange way, it was a pleasure to listen to.

"...Somebody called you on the phone, said there was a *rape*? I got that call first night I was *out*! Who the hell are *you*?!"

A black man in his early 40s dressed in business attire walked quickly past without acknowledging him, and Nutter Butter flinched like he'd just dodged a blow.

"Step up on me again, nigger!" he yelped, straightening up and squaring his shoulders. "Step. Up. On. Me. Again. Step up on me again, and I'll kick your ass." The man ignored him, which brought Nutter Butter out from behind his carts in pursuit—though he maintained a safe distance of several feet. When his latest nemesis joined the other commuters under the signpost for the Rapid line, Nutter Butter held his position.

"Wake me up again and see what happens. Go on. You just try it. And stay away from my 40!"

The group waiting at the Rapid stop were already uncomfortable, and his sudden penetration of their general proximity did nothing to soothe their jangled nerves. He wasn't just dirty and crazed; now he was targeting *them*. The savage was loose!

"You're a rapist. You're a murderer. You're everything under the goddamn *Golden Rule!*"

At last, a Rapid bus pulled up, packed to the walls. Not that it mattered to those waiting; faced with the prospect of even another ten minutes on the street with an honest-to-God raving maniac, they couldn't squeeze in fast enough.

"Get in there with the rest of them, you big ugly motherfucker!" he yelled at me. "Get on that bus!"

He sized me up a moment.

"Oh, are you the boss man? Huh? I'll come over there and kick your ass, boss man!"

I did nothing, and he stepped back in triumph.

"Boss man," he spat. "Let's see you boss something *now!*" He turned and strutted unsteadily back to his shopping carts.

On the next bus west, a middle-aged Mexican day laborer with a graying moustache and paint-spattered pants was wearing a T-shirt with a drawing of a frog seated at a bar.

The animal was slumped forward, its eyelids heavy. The cartoon bar was littered with cartoon spills and empty cartoon glasses, and a random series of exotic punctuation marks floated in a halo around his cartoon head.

At the top, bubble letters spelled out the phrase *Soy el bebedor designado*—"I am the designated drinker"—but the laborer wasn't drunk or drinking, and he didn't seem to be in an especially festive mood. In fact, he looked tired and ready to pack it in; but odds were he was only just beginning his trip to a job he wouldn't be returning from for ten or twelve hard hours.

His round belly strained against the thinning white cotton of his worn shirt, and both suggested a long term of service as *bebedor designado*. He let out a deep sigh and turned his face to the window, squinting against the glare of the morning.

As a rule, cartoon animals on novelty T-shirts tend to be having more fun than the people wearing them.

bust a move

A FRIEND from work had given me a lift most of the way
home, but when he missed his turn, he had to drop me off
on Hollywood Boulevard in front of the Chinese Theater,
midway between two bus stops. I walked in the direction of
the stop farther along the route, figuring if the bus arrived
in the meantime, at least I'd be ahead of it.

The sidewalk in front of the theater was already blocked
off in anticipation of a movie premiere later that evening.
Though it was nothing more than a cheap roll duct-taped
to the dirty sidewalk, I was instinctively considerate of
the red carpet, walking in the street as I passed, keeping
close to the curb. Traffic wasn't heavy, and enough orange
cones had been set up in the street to keep it from feeling
particularly hazardous.

"Sir! Sir!" someone called.

Two young men in dark polyester suits trotted over from
their post a few feet away, tight plastic coils dangling from
their ears. By getting out of the car in the middle of the
block, I had inadvertently bypassed their security gauntlet.

"Excuse me sir, are you Press?" one asked, eyeing the
canvas bag hanging from my shoulder.

"No."

"Well, I'm afraid you can't go that way. The sidewalk is
closed off."

"I'm in the street."

"Sorry sir, you'll have to go around."

"Go around?"

"Yes sir. Where are you headed?"

I pointed to the corner. "The bus stop, right there."

"I'm sorry, the sidewalk is closed. You'll have to go
around."

It was typical Hollywood insanity. That it was at least
an hour, probably two, before any real premiere activity
would even *begin* to begin made no difference; anything
to do with the merest handful of celebrities trying to sell
something would always assume top priority, outweighing
any inconvenience to everyone else.

Now at the tail-end of a lengthy commute home from a hard day at an unstable job working for a bunch of pricks, it's quite a thing to be chased away from a bus stop so as not to disturb the preparation of a balloon party for overprivileged assholes.

The whole thing hardly seemed worth fighting over. But then, for the few yards I had left to go to reach my stop, it hardly seemed worth their trouble to redirect me. I kept my impulse to argue in check. What was the point? Turning me around was precisely what these guys were making nine bucks an hour to do. I quit the fight early. It didn't matter.

"So how do I get around this bullshit?"

"Right through there and through the stores, sir," one of them said, indicating that I should go into the mall complex that surrounded the theater and wind my way through the maze of shops inside in order to emerge thirty feet from where I was now standing.

"You've got to be fucking kidding me."

"Sorry sir, but...."

I already knew. The sidewalk was *closed*.

DOWN the block from the prefab security gates, a large crowd—seven to ten deep—had gathered, but not for the movie premiere. Instead, the focus was a single performer, and no celebrity: a lean, shirtless black man in a patchy beard and old sneakers, breakdancing for change. I caught sight of him through the crowd, frozen in a half-handstand.

Then, as whistles and beats blasted from a battered old boom box, he spun off on his shoulder in a move that had everyone whooping and applauding. I hadn't seen people so enthralled by breakdancing since the '80s.

Some yards away from the throng, at the Hollywood and Highland bus stop, a small group of kids from Inglewood stood around a lamppost, flirting with a tall, slim homegirl. She wore white spiked heels and a black belly shirt, and had a teenager's spotty complexion. The boys were fifteen years old at most, but they were tall and carried themselves with an outsized determination to be seen as harder than their years.

The 212 to Inglewood pulled to the curb. Its passengers

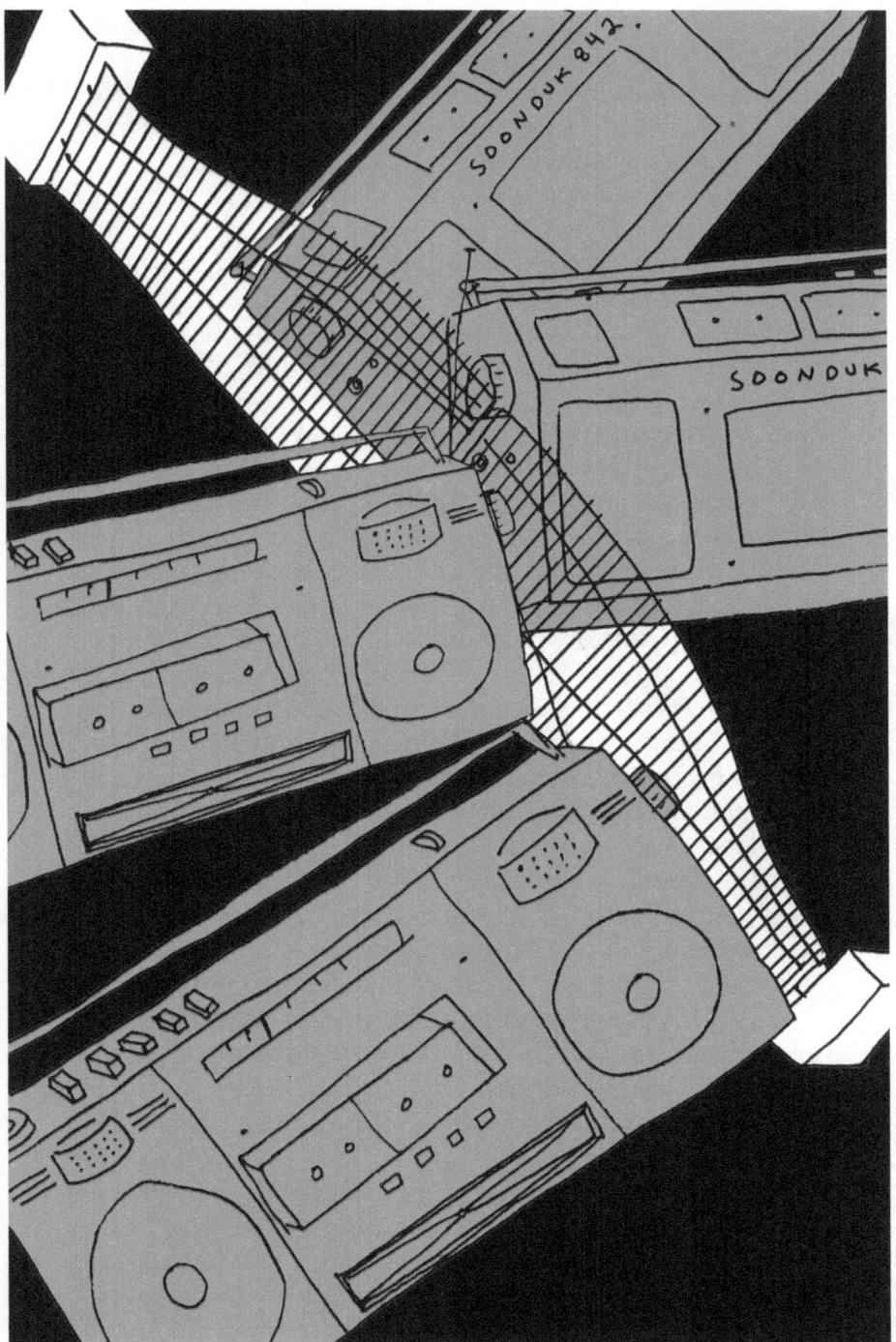

disembarked, and the group around the lamppost lined up
to board, save two: the girl, who was waiting for another
bus, and a kid in a do-rag and white Tupac tee at least two
sizes bigger than his small frame needed. He stood at the
back doors of the bus, signaling for someone inside to push
them open so he could sneak in.

"What you're doing is illegal!" a thick, wet voice barked.
"Get away from there!"

The kid and I both turned in the direction of the voice.
The accuser was a small white guy with stooped shoulders
and five o'clock shadow beginning to shade his soft chin.
His dark red hair was cropped close and fading fast, but
there was still enough to compliment the coppery wool that
sprouted from under the back of his collar. The thick lenses
of his heavy glasses were fishbowls for his milky eyes,
and distorted them to unfortunate comic effect; the heavy
frames were secured by a clean white string that dangled
awkwardly down either side of his face. He kept an orderly
appearance, but his dark blue slacks and Oxford were faded
with wear. He looked dusty and scuffed, like an old shoe.

"Who you talking to?" The kid snapped back at him.

"You're trying to sneak onto that bus without paying
the fare. And the driver..." He paused in mid-sentence, as if
correcting a wrong turn. He spoke with a heavy tongue, and
I noticed he wore a small, flesh-colored plastic nautilus in
each ear.

"...It's *illegal!*" he continued. "And I will call 911 right
now if you don't stop what you're doing." He moved his hand
over the bulge in the breast pocket of his shirt, making it
plain that he had a cell phone and was prepared to use it.

"Call whoever you want, *bitch!*" the kid popped back,
coming down hard on the B. He threw a hostile look my way
too, whoever the fuck I was.

"You wanna call somebody? Call 'em, I don't give a *fuck*,"
he told us both.

When you square off against an animal in the wild, they
say you should show no fear, and open your arms so you
appear larger than you really are. And that's what this kid
did, getting in the older man's face and throwing his arms
out at odd angles. Or maybe he was just mimicking in-your-
face-motherfucker gestures familiar from a thousand music

videos and hip-hop photo shoots.

"Hm? Hm? Hm?" he taunted.

Another of the kid's friends circled in a supporting pantomime, launching his own series of bends and gestures, baiting the man behind his back. Their swoops and movements were an elaborate choreography of aggression, a war dance on either side of the small, immobile white man.

Despite the bizarre menace of his circumstances, the older man neither backed down nor appeared intimidated by any of it. It may have been that there just wasn't time; the conflict ended abruptly when the kids' friends called out to get on the bus before it left. The kid popped his neck at his antagonist—a warning strike—and he and his partner skipped off to join the rest of their crew as paying customers.

A moment later, the 217 South arrived and the remaining commuters moved closer to the curb to meet it. A prim woman in her 50s stepped into an open space near the stoop-shouldered man. Taking that as some sign of solidarity, he launched into a full debriefing.

"I was ready to call 911 and have that bunch of..." He paused, seemingly censoring himself. "...*Jokers* arrested! They are in violation of penal code, uh... I don't know what it is for the bus. But they would have had to pay two hundred and fifty dollars each. And forty hours of community service!" He sounded each syllable of community with such precision it was like a new word.

We all boarded, and I took a seat toward the front, across the aisle from the girl the kids on the other bus had been flirting with. She sat next to an only slightly older girl, who also wore a tight black T-shirt. Hers had glittered cursive that read,

"Hmmm... Let's see..."

Then, underneath, in bigger, block capitals:

"Whatever."

I noticed the white gothic lettering on the younger girl's shirt.

"Angel Baby," it said.

the dark knight returns

THE 750 is a bus in the Rapid line, and some drivers take
the designation more literally than others. This one did.

The bus was full, and I was one of a handful standing
as we burned down Ventura Boulevard heading west. The
increased speed didn't appear to demand any additional
concentration on the driver's part, and he maintained a
cordial conversation with one of the passengers about the
new Batman movie he'd seen over the weekend.

The passenger—another middle-aged black man—
wore a wispy goatee and dark sunglasses. He was in the
conversation seat, closest to the door and facing the driver.
He sat at an angle, leaning in to hear the driver more
clearly, while a large woman without a seat stood in the
aisle directly between them. Though she obscured the men's
view of each other, her being there interfered with their
discussion no more than the noise of the bus did; while she
stood between them, bored and staring off into space, they
just spoke around her.

"He's in *shape!*" the driver called.

"Who?"

"Chris Bale. The guy who's the new Batman."

"Oh, yeah." The passenger stroked his small beard.
"Well, three months before they even start they send you off
to get you ready. Training. You can't be doing that kind of
action looking all crazy."

"Gary Oldman is in it, too."

"Who?"

"Gary Oldman."

"Ah, the old character man," he replied knowingly.

Someone pulled the cord to signal their street, and the
bus lurched to a stop so hard I almost lost my footing; the
iced coffee I'd bought for the trip left me with only one hand
to hold the rail, and I narrowly avoided tumbling into the
lap of a large woman in sweatpants—nothing either of us
would have enjoyed.

The jolt was like on a cartoon bus, with sharp
punctuation marks blowing out from under the squealing

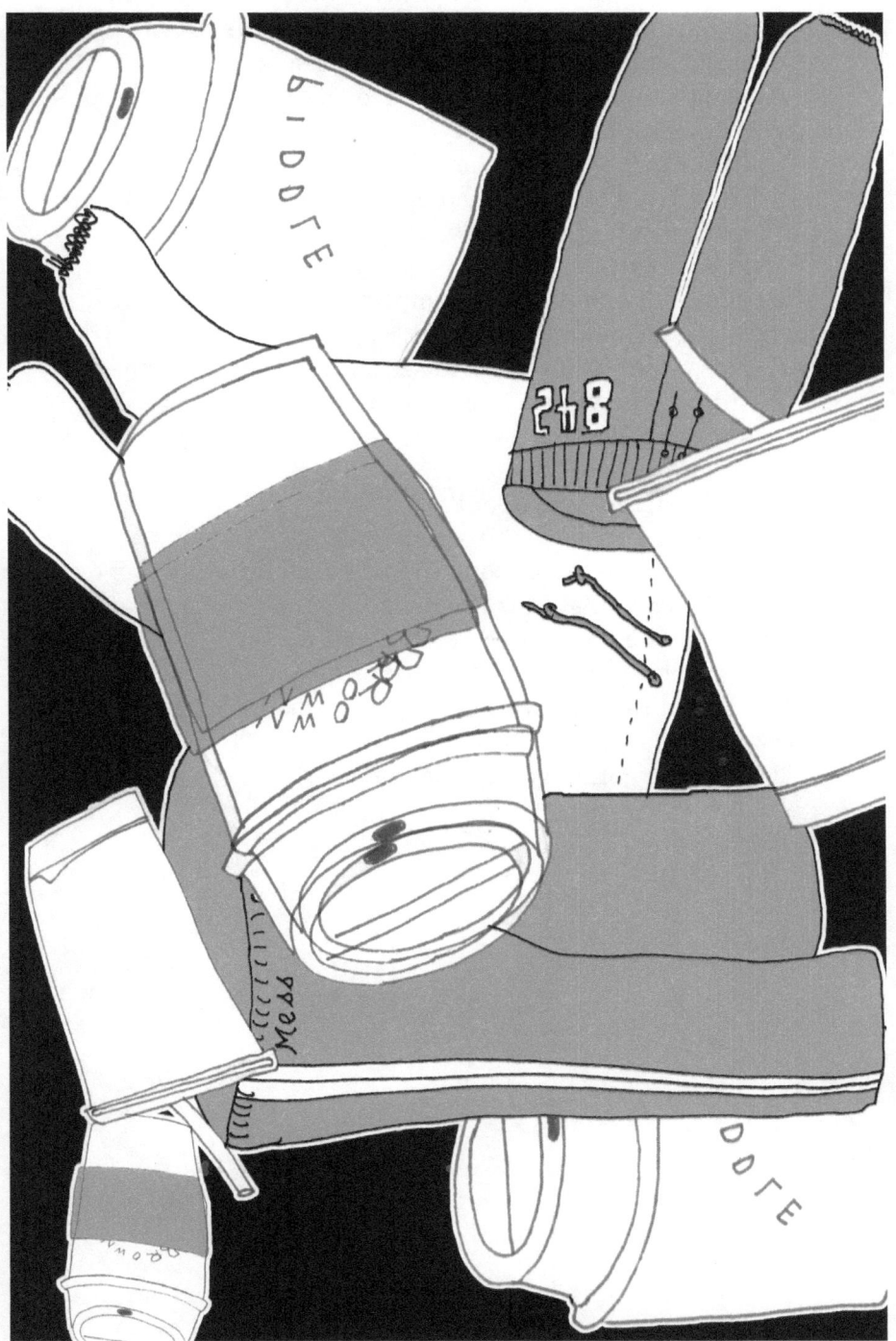

front tires, the back end mule-kicking before settling like a spent accordion into great speckled dust clouds. In the air, the chaotic clanking of pots and pans loose in a box.

Passengers exited and boarded, doors closed and the bus jerked back into high gear. My stop was next.

"And the girl is good," the driver continued. "She looks *good*, Katie Holmes. She be holding it down."

"Tom Cruise's girl," the passenger acknowledged.

"She be holding it *down*."

He made the point as if prompting him to agree; but if it was bait, his friend didn't take it.

"I guess I definitely have to see that Wednesday, then."

"Yeah, and now I got to go get myself some Bat-gear."

"Some what?"

"Some Bat-GEAR."

"Oh, you all serious about it!"

The driver shrugged. "It was *good!*"

The bus jumped to a stop, and the back doors swung out to the curb. The blast of traffic noise through the open doors drowned out the passenger's response.

"What's that you said?" the driver asked.

His friend raised his voice, making a point of speaking each word clearly.

"I said, you gonna get a *cape* too, bro?"

rolling in the cracker barrel

WILLIAM drove the 842 almost to the corner before stopping, leaving plenty of room behind him for any of the other three buses that shared the timetable, should they appear.

A very old man in a military surplus jacket and washed-out blue jeans climbed on ahead of me; he wasn't someone I recognized as a regular. He lingered at the farebox, then positioned himself to claim the open seat closest to the door.

But with people that old, even a simple act like taking a seat on the bus becomes a process, to be executed in stages. And while the old man hovered in a holding pattern, a nearby woman about his age got up quickly and moved away from him. William didn't miss that, and jumped up from his seat, turning on the old man.

"Hold on, hold on!" William said. "Don't sit down. Are you wet?"

The man looked confused.

"Are you WET?" William asked again, raising his voice.

The man patted his front and rear, as though checking for a wallet. Stains on the seat of his light blue jeans had created a sepia-toned psychedelic happening.

"Not wet," he replied in a thick Eastern European accent.

"Where are you getting off?"

"Hah?"

"WHERE ARE YOU GETTING OFF?"

"I don't understand," he said firmly, no question in his voice.

"Where are you going?"

"Ah. *Senta* Monica Boulevard."

William shook his head, returned to his seat behind the wheel and drove on.

"You saw I had to make him check himself," he said to me after the old man had exited a few stops later. "I ain't gonna have that." He smiled a little. "There's one woman who rides, she makes him smell like roses."

"She a real fragrant lady?" I asked.

"All the drivers know her. They call her *Baby Girl*. Heh

heh heh heh."

"I know what you mean," interrupted a small, skinny white guy in his 40s, scuttling into a vacant seat down front to join the conversation.

He looked like a piece of frayed wire, with a head a size too big for his shoulders and a sandpaper complexion. I'd run into him before on the commute home. I remembered him pulling from a pint bottle in a wrinkled paper bag, smelling like a cheap pack of cigarettes somebody'd smoked in the rain.

The first time I'd seen him, he'd pulled up a seat and began grousing about how the girl who'd just got off was cute, but Jesus Christ did she talk too much! Since I was the one she'd been talking with, he made it easy to file him under "asshole" for future reference.

"I work construction," he continued, "and this one guy, one of the brothers"—he used the term with obvious contempt—"was always hangin' around. We're tryin' to keep an eye on him and all, but, you know, we're *workin'*. We'd run him off, and he'd come right back!" He wheezed out a chuckle. "Yeah, we used to throw pebbles at him, little rocks, from up on the second floor," he snorted.

Realizing he was the only one laughing, he backpedaled a little. "I guess it wasn't the nicest thing to do, but he wouldn't go away." He frowned at the lack of audience response. Fresh out of small talk, he put an unlit cigarette in his mouth for when he got off.

A young white collar-and-tie we'd picked up in West Hollywood leaned conspiratorially into the discussion.

"Well, there's a guy at my work, he hangs around the front of the building. He's had both legs amputated, and one day he just…" (his voice dropped to near silence, apparently out of courtesy) "…*shit* there. We called the city. We told them, and they said they'd take care of it. They charged us two hundred and sixty dollars to clean it up! Biohazard."

I checked his expression to see if he was joking—not about the amputee, but about the call. I couldn't imagine someone calling the city to rinse a turd off the sidewalk.

"Hell, if the city's charging $260 a pop, I'm gonna spring for a garden hose and follow this guy's wheelchair around!" another passenger called, joining the party. "Could be a promising career move!"

Most of them chuckled, and it seemed everyone was eager to share their tales of Wacky Homeless They Had Known. But the war stories all came across like guilty confessions in the telling.

Somehow William's never did. Driving the bus as long as he had, he had more and better stories than any of them, but he'd long since clammed up. Watching him silently watching the road, I had the distinct impression he was in no hurry to turn the 7:20 run into a Town Meeting on wheels.

It was hard to blame him; you want to choose your company when you can.

pay the man

"LAST week was payday, and the checks are supposed to be there by lunchtime. I'm usually done by 1:30, but here it was 2:00 and there were still no checks! A lot of people got direct deposit, but I don't. I asked when the checks were coming in, and they said maybe by 5. I wasn't gonna wait around all day, so I asked this lady Claudia to pick up my check for me when she got off her shift.

"She say she live in Venice; that's a lot closer for me to get to than driving all the way back to the yard, in Sylmar. I didn't have her number, so I gave her my cell number. I told her to call me when she gets home, and I'd come by and get my check.

"I went home, but then I thought I lost my phone; I couldn't find it anywhere. And that was the number I gave Claudia to call me at! So I got my regular phone from the house and called my cell phone to see if I could hear it ringing, but I remembered I had it set to 'vibrate,' so I wouldn't be able to hear it anyway. Real quick, I called the number for work. I told them I lost my phone and could they give Claudia this other number, my home number? They said okay.

"I had to call Verizon to cancel the phone because, you know, people get hold of your phone and they start running it up. Verizon told me, 'Well, the last call we show for you was at 3:24.' I said that's good, 'cause I knew that was me. So they shut it down.

"A few minutes after that, I went out to my car and I started feeling around under the seats. BAM! There's the phone, way back there under the front seat! I called Verizon again to get it turned back on, and they gave me all these numbers I had to punch into the phone to get it to work. Then I called work again and told them, 'Disregard that message from before!' They said okay.

"Pretty soon it's after 5, and I still haven't heard anything. And I had asked Claudia to pick up this other lady's check, too; I said I would drop it off for her. So now this other lady's calling me.

"She says, 'Who's this Claudia anyway? How you know she's not out *partying* with all that money?' 'Cause three people's checks is some money.

"I said, 'Don't worry about her! Claudia's a good person, she's good as gold. She's been there as long as I have; I'm not worried about any hanky-panky from Claudia.'

"But then I was thinking maybe she might have tried to get in touch with me when my phone was off. When you don't hear from somebody who's holding your pay... After a while, you start to wonder what's up!"

"Sure," I agreed. "You're talking about your paycheck; that's your lifeline, there."

"Yeah, and money makes people do strange things. You never know how somebody's gonna be. Like I tell my girl, you have to be careful! She don't have direct deposit either; when she gets paid, she just goes to the bank and cashes her check. I tell her, you cash your check, then you go off to the ladies' room or something... You leave your purse behind, somebody could take your money. And once it's gone, you can't do anything about it. It's not like somebody stealing a check, where at least you're a little protected.

"That's what happened at this other job I had before, I worked with this guy Toney. He was a supervisor. Well, not really a supervisor. He was what they called a lead man; he was *kind* of a supervisor. He was a real likable person. And this was a small office, only maybe eight people. A small office like that, everybody thinks they know each other.

"He must have owed a lot of money, and I guess the

creditors was calling on the phone, calling him at his place of business. One day at work he got brought into the office—'What's all this about?' Toney said, 'Oh, I'll take care of that when I get paid this Friday.' Well, he took care of it, all right!

"That Friday, two of the ladies had cashed their checks at lunch, and he stole the money right out of their pocketbooks when they weren't looking. He emptied all the money out of petty cash, too. Come Monday, he just didn't show up; he never came back to work again.

"Anyway, I phoned up this other woman I work with. She said she had Claudia's number and gave it to me—her home number. So I called her house and her kid answered. I said, 'Where your momma at?' He said she wasn't home yet. I started to wonder if maybe Claudia *was* out partying! I said, 'You got any way to reach her? Call her and tell her to call me back, it's important.' He said he would tell her. Now I was really starting to worry.

"A little while later, my phone rang. It was Claudia calling me back; she had just got in. Turns out, the checks didn't show up from the main office until something like 7:00. And then there was fifty or sixty people waiting in line ahead of her to get theirs before she gotta drive all the way home from Sylmar. Made me feel a little bad I'd been chasing her down all day.

"When I went to pick up my check from her, I told her I was sorry, because for a minute I had doubted her myself. She looked real tired. I gave her a hug; it was all right.

"'Happy New Year,' she told me." He was wistful.

The bus' front tire bit down on the lip of a stray hubcap, sending it skipping noisily across the asphalt like a bottle top. It landed against the curb with a loud, tin clank. William turned to the Asian lady seated by the door.

"That side of the bus just fell off," he said gravely. She laughed.

"So everything ended up all right for everybody?" I asked.

"Later on," he frowned, "the other lady called me after I dropped off her check. I guess they went through some other service to get the checks this time, 'cause it was on a different kind of paper.

"She goes, 'Do your check look *funny* to you?'"

birthday boy

"You got anything going this weekend?"

"Naw, not really," William said. "I'm looking forward to resting. I'd be glad to be at home, but my girl, she always wants to go out on the weekend, you know, go dancing or something." He shook his head. "She says, 'You don't want to take me to a club?' And I tell her, 'That's like bringing sand to the beach!'" He laughed. "The clubs, they all either too young or too old. I'll take her someplace nice for our anniversary—that's on the 14th. Wait, what's today?"

"The 11th."

"Okay, so the 14th, that's Monday."

"She's into that kind of thing? She gets all excited?"

"Oh yeah, she's like that." He dropped his voice. "Not me!

"There's this one guy I knew, he went to jail. And when his birthday came up, he said, 'Hey, what are you guys gonna do for my birthday?' They said, 'Fuck your *birfday*, we in the *pen*!'" he cackled. "I guess he thought they was gonna lay out a spread or something!

"Eventually he got out, and guess what happened? While he was away, his girl had took up with some other guy. He found out about it and went looking for her. He waited until she was coming out of some place and BAM! He shot her."

"So he killed his girlfriend and went right back in?"

"He didn't kill her; he just shot her up."

"They'll still put you away for trying," I said.

"Mm hm. Sent him off for life."

"Well, I hope this time he remembered the party hats."

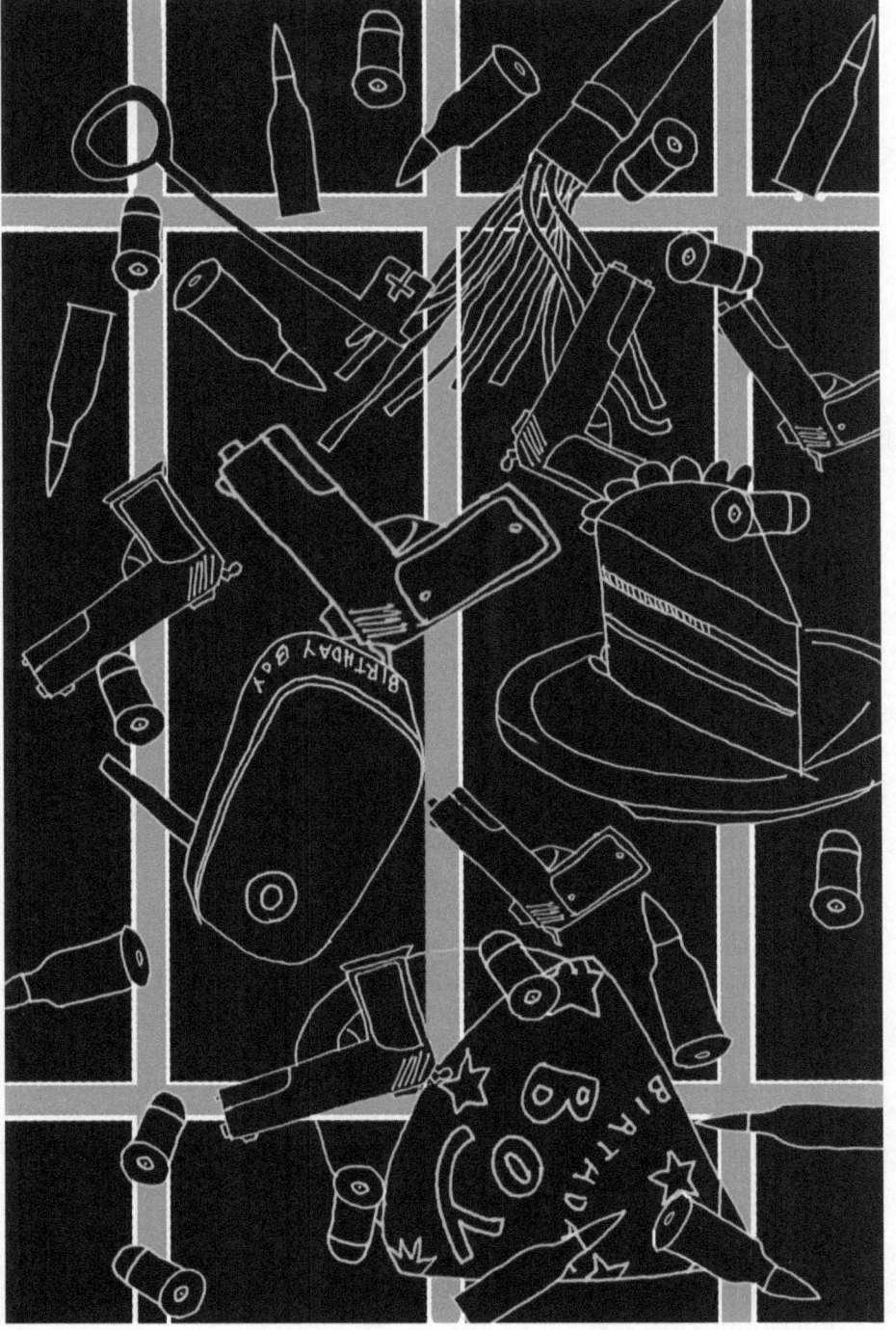

heroes aren't hard to find

IT WAS a Sunday afternoon in late June, which meant more tourists than usual on Hollywood Boulevard. And all those people meant a long day for Spiderman and Spongebob Squarepants.

It wasn't especially warm for midsummer, but being covered from head to toe in a cheap polyester bodysuit will raise the temperature even on a mild day. Technically, Spongebob had more breathing room in his costume, but at the end of the day he was still a man inside a refrigerator box wrapped in a scavenged yellow blanket, and he was effectively insulated from even the momentary relief of any passing breeze.

What did foreign tourists unfamiliar with Spongebob's domestic celebrity make of him? This strolling monster with its maniacal fixed expression, a furry block of psychotic cheese in short pants?

Though they were traveling without children, a group of Pakistani sightseers in sporty clothes approached Spiderman with cameras and Spongebob went on his way, waving a genial farewell to his cartoon colleague.

The family gathered to pose around the dollar store superhero, and he assumed an action stance. It was one of five in his repertoire, and the one best suited for pictures with large groups.

"Make it seem as though he is rescuing you," ordered one of the amateur photographers in a clipped accent. Spiderman straightened up and reassumed his position while a second cameraman documented the entire process with a compact video recorder.

"Okay, thank you," the still photographer announced several shutter clicks later. The group broke up, turning away from Spiderman without acknowledgement.

"Uh, I work on tips," he called out meekly. He pointed to a blue fanny pack incongruously slung over his crotch.

"Give him a few bucks," the still photographer said, waving them off as he occupied himself with some detail of his camera.

There was a hint of annoyance in the way the family rummaged through their purses once the moment's entertainment had been thoroughly exhausted. They seemed eager to leave this spent occasion behind them and move quickly on to whatever was next, unsparing in their determination to wring the last drop of amusement from every single minute of their vacation.

Spiderman accepted the few singles appreciatively. He rolled them up to the size of a cigarette and opened the mouth of his pouch just enough to push them through the teeth before zipping it closed. Though his costume sagged noticeably in spots, he revealed a severe wedgie as he turned to go, and it provided an alarming definition to his rear.

He walked off, a slump coming into his posture as he began to slip out of character. He was going home, but remained in full costume despite the discomfort. The Boulevard superheroes made a point of not removing their masks in public, and besides, another tourist family could appear on the way, and that might lead to another photo opportunity. It would mean a later subway home, but it would also mean another couple of dollars.

Walking east on Hollywood Boulevard, his departure was somehow less than heroic.

NEAR the sign listing the several buses that ran along Hollywood Boulevard, a young black girl with tightly-braided hair yelled across the wide street at ear-shattering volume:

"Bran-DON! BRANNNNDON!!!"

Across the traffic, on the opposite sidewalk, three kids about her age craned their necks to the source of the shouting. Two wore oversized sports jerseys and the third wore a dark polo shirt from one of the fast-food cafes on the Boulevard. All three waved back at her.

"Get back to WORK, Brandon! BRAN-DON! Get back to WORK!"

A small crowd of the girl's friends gathered around her, and she spontaneously began to lead them in a synchronized chant-and-dance, like a scene out of some lost urban musical.

"*A! B! C! D-E-F-G-H!*"

Weaving in and out of each other, they bobbed, popped and threw arms in a gangsta drumline stepshow.

"*I-J-K-L! M! N! O! P!*"

They fired off letters with flawless coordination and a military precision only appropriate for this twenty-six gun salute to good phonics.

"*Q-R-S! T-U-V!*"

The compelling, surreal quality of the performance was almost enough to make you forget to wonder what might have led to the creation of such a routine in the first place.

"*W! X! Y! Z!*

"*We the ALPHABET Gang!*"

As the kids hi- and lo-fived, the young girl took her place in front of her friends. Center stage, she folded her arms in a gesture of finality.

"*A-B-C,* nigguh!"

interpretations

"I KNOW you!"

Smokey's raspy voice was a Bronx cheer from a bed of gravel, and he was loud, even for the bus.

He did know me. Or at least, I knew him. We'd shared a ride a few months back. His small talk took frequent turns for the bizarre and he delivered streams of non sequiturs and utter nonsense with the force and certainty of a man speaking plainly, with points to make. He didn't have to try very hard to make an impression.

"You used to be a cook," he insisted, regarding me warmly. "With Jerry and Ray. At the cooking school, in Ohio."

"Nope. I never was a cook in Ohio."

"Must be a different person then," he decided. He turned away, and we were strangers again.

His head and face were overgrown with wiry curls patched with gray. Behind the sagebrush on his cheeks, he gnawed gently on a little wad of paper—the sheer wrapper

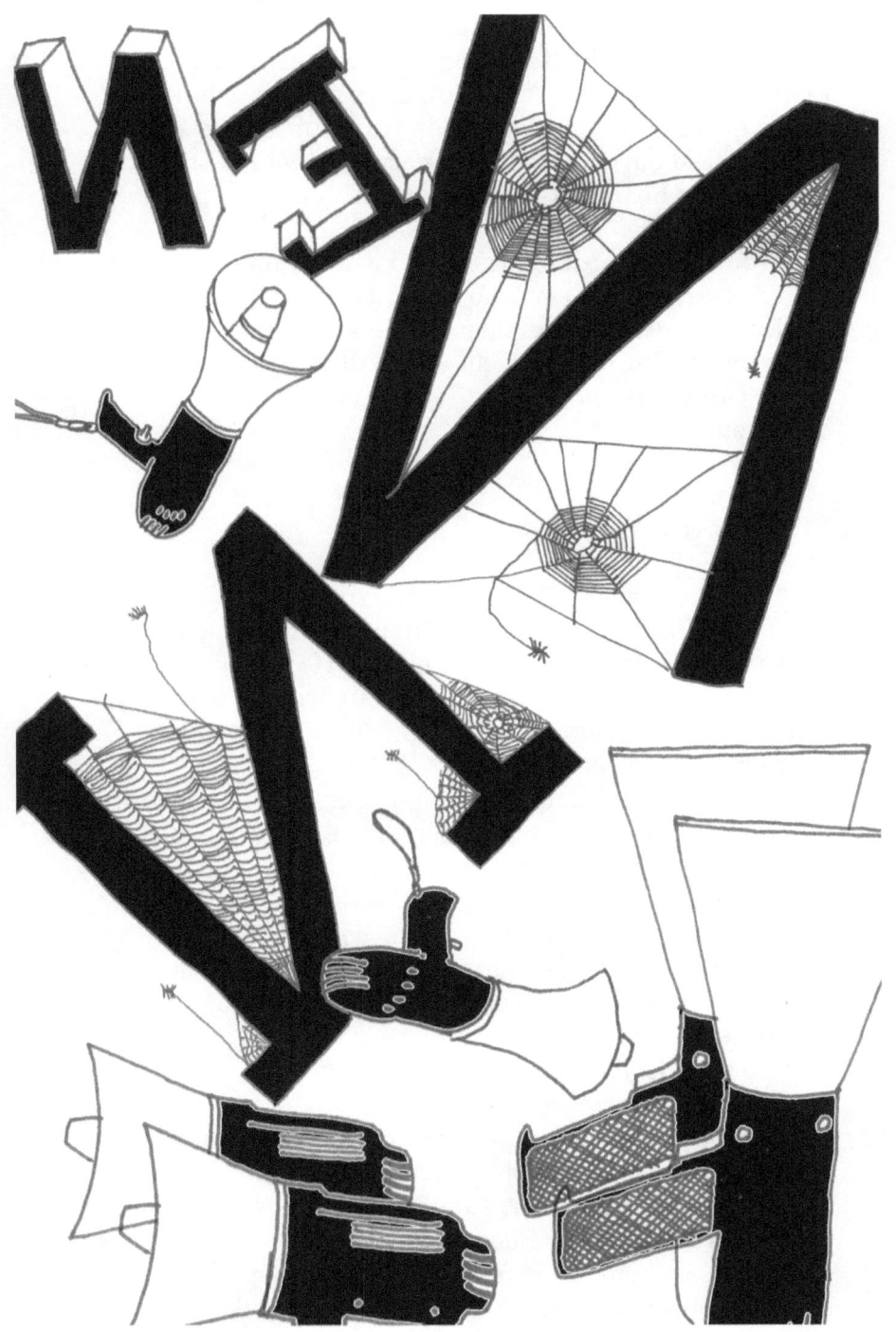

from a drinking straw. The last remaining stub stuck to his bottom lip like a flattened cigarette butt.

Chewing quietly, he stared straight ahead, eyebrows raised nonchalantly. A big man, tall and broad, he was disheveled in his chocolate nylon tracksuit, and the canvas ball cap he'd parked high on his afro had tented there, bringing his head to a peak. It gave him the profile of an amiable yeti.

"You went to cooking school?" I asked him.

"That was years ago," he said dismissively, unwilling to discuss the matter further. "I had a clothing store in Long Beach. On 103rd Street and Willow. It was ah, ah, it was called *Interpretations*. It was like, ah, the Men's Wearhouse."

"Oh yeah?"

"It was called Interpretations," he repeated.

"It's a good name."

"I know."

"Was it expensive?" I asked. "To run it?"

"Pepto Bizmo," he said, brightening. "That's what it was. Pepto Bizmo, gives you a hairy chest!" He leaned closer, pulling down the neck of his T-shirt to proudly expose the salt-and-pepper thatch that bloomed under his collar. "You got hair on your chest?"

I opened an extra button on my shirt and showed him.

"Ha!" he barked. "You got some, too! Pepto Bizmo!" He reached over and enthusiastically shook my hand in woolly camaraderie.

"I just got out of the shower," he continued. "I put the key under the mat. My mat, it's, it's a balloon. It's a *blow-up* balloon. I have to keep it from floating away. Ha!"

He studied my face.

"Do you, do you make wristwatches?"

"Do I make wristwatches? No."

"You, you don't make wristwatches!" he laughed. "You make wall clocks! Ha! You make *wall clocks*!"

A sharp bang rang out suddenly a few rows ahead of us. One of the upper windows—smaller, horizontal slats of safety glass, about three feet long—had snapped loose from its moorings on the wall and dangled at a crooked angle over the adjacent seats.

I recognized the girl in that row. Tall for a Mexican girl, and slim. Not much in the way of curves, but nice to look at and she knew it. She caught the bus at my stop, and never talked to anyone.

She pushed at the disjointed window but couldn't budge it, and there were no open seats for her to move to. I got up and made my way down the aisle, clasping the parallel handrails like monkey bars against the rocking of the bus.

"Here."

Using both hands, I gripped the window by its aluminum trim. A firm diagonal shove put it back into alignment, and a second push set it back into its frame. The small pneumatic hinges on either side of the panel wheezed softly with the smooth closing of the window, and I fastened the clip at the top, locking it shut.

"There you go."

I'd fixed it—at least temporarily—but she didn't thank me. That surprised me. Maybe it stemmed from a sense of entitlement I thought I'd picked up on from her before. Or maybe it was my choice of company, and whatever assumptions she may have made about that.

I returned to the back of the bus and took my seat across from Smokey. He didn't move, but his eyes slowly traveled from me to the girl to her now-repaired window.

"Did you..." he began to ask.

I offered a small smile of resignation. "Hey, I tried," I said, a shrug in my voice.

He looked at me quizzically before resuming his question.

"...Did you ever see the *Fish Man*? That movie?" He mimed a breast stroke, using flattened palms to part imaginary waters in front of him.

"You mean The Creature?" I asked him.

"The Fish Creature?"

"No, *The Creature from the Black Lagoon*."

"Izzat it? The Black Lagoon?"

"Yeah. They made three of them. Back in the '50s."

"Smart," he said, nodding his approval. "Smart."

treasures of tutankhamen

I WAS surprised to see William behind the wheel of the 842 that Friday. Mostly since he'd been on a different schedule lately, but also because I'd been going to work earlier and hadn't seen much of him all week.

"You doing anything nice this weekend?" I asked him.

"Nothing special. Just your standard R&R," he said. "I might go to LACMA tonight." LACMA was the Los Angeles County Museum of Art, a key point of convergence for the wine and cheese crowd.

"You gonna see King Tut?" That was the big exhibit trumpeted from banner advertisements hanging from streetlamps all over town.

"Naw, they got those free jazz concerts on Fridays," he reminded me.

"Oh yeah," I said.

"I been to the Getty. It's seven dollars, and that gets you into everything," he said, implying LACMA was no such bargain. "But the Getty, the paintings they have there.... It's not emotional kind of painting. It's 'This is Peter.' 'This is Paul.' 'Here's The Last Supper.' It's people like Rembrandt. Their masterpieces."

"Right, right." *Rembrandt's Late Religious Portraits.* Those ads were on the streetlamps, too.

"I was going to see King Tut last week when I was there, though. At LACMA."

"You didn't go in?"

"I thought about it. It was nine dollars to get in. Later I read in the paper that you could get tickets for a hundred dollars. V.I.P. tickets."

"What's a V.I.P. ticket?"

"It means you can go in and out anytime you want. But they make out like it be a mob scene over there!"

"It's not?"

"Naw! It's like going to the movies. You go up to the box office, you pay for your ticket and you go in. At the window, they have a nine dollar ticket and a thirty dollar ticket."

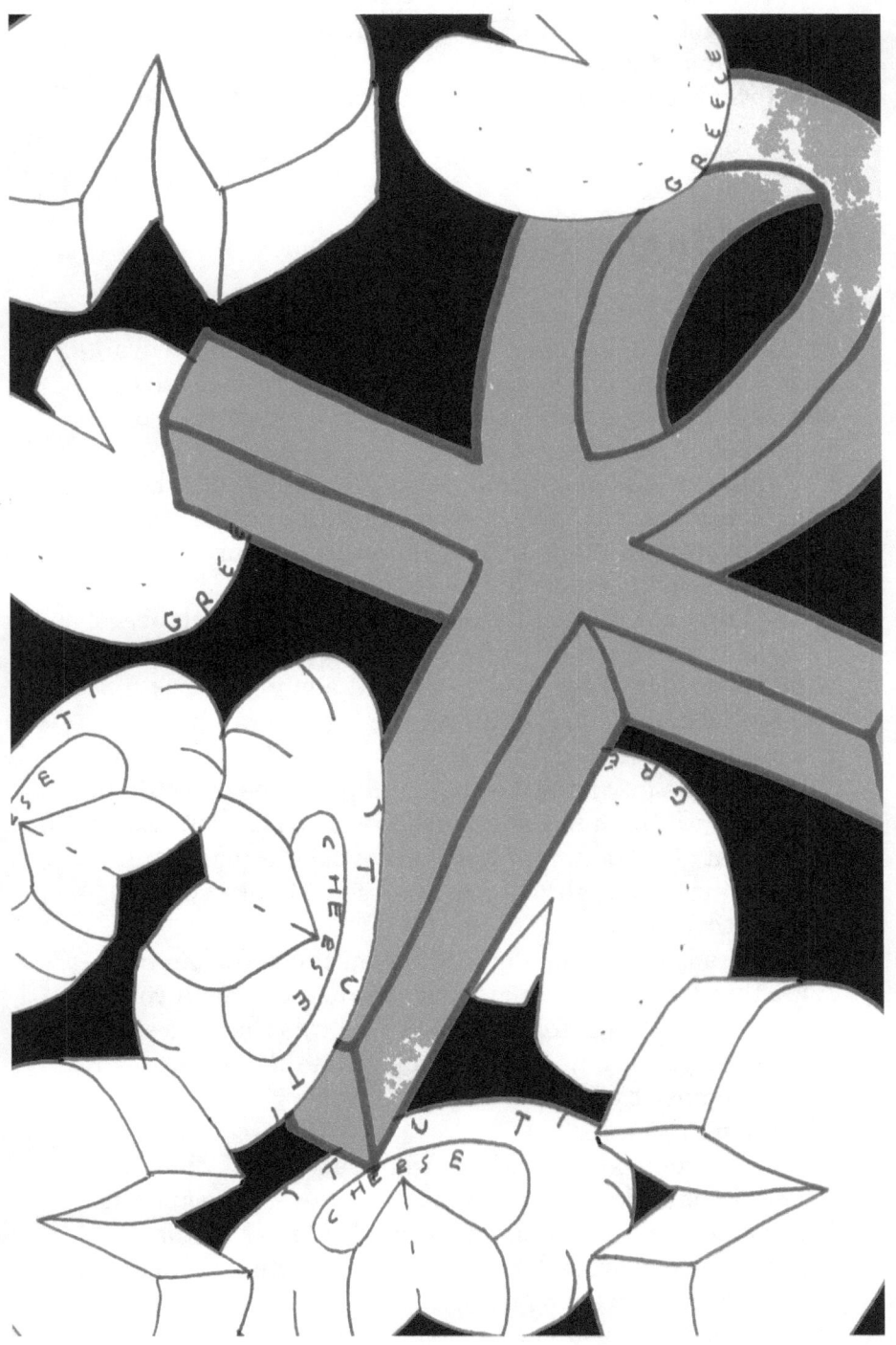

"What does a thirty dollar ticket get you?"

"You get to see more," William shrugged.

"So what'd you end up going with?"

"I went to the Japanese Museum down the way. For *free*."

wild kingdom

MY CONNECTION, a Rapid bus, had passed while the 842 was stuck at a red light. There'd be at least a ten minute wait for the next one, so I hung around the bus to shoot the breeze with William. We sat parked on a side street, on break before his next run south.

"Did you hear about that movie," I asked him, "that documentary about the guy who lived with bears? He camped out with them for thirteen years—no problems— then one year they ended up killing him."

"I didn't see that, but yeah, you can't mess with bears! I saw this show, I don't know if it was a documentary or what, where this bear took a swing at a guy and took his leg right off! Then the bear grabbed the leg and ran back into the forest with it."

"Well this guy knew how dangerous the bears could be; he lived with them in the woods for years. He even saw bears that got too hungry kill their own cubs for food. It didn't matter, though. He was obsessed. He pretty much wanted to *be* a bear."

"Bears is wild animals! Maybe you can train 'em to do some things, like in a circus, but that doesn't mean you can just move in. People forget that. There was that one story where people were having their picture taken with a bear, you remember that?"

"I don't think so."

"I can't remember if he had a muzzle... Yeah, I think he did have a muzzle. This bear was looking over here and this lady sat down next to him. She wanted to take a picture. When he turned around, he saw that lady sitting there and it startled him. He went *off* on her!"

"What, he clawed her?"

"Well, I think maybe he had his claws removed...."

"They're still really strong."

"I'm pretty sure it was a Asian lady. You know how they are always getting their cameras out, taking pictures of things." He shook his head. "That's like that Jane Goodall, with the monkeys. That's what they say happened to her."

"Not Jane Goodall," I insisted. "She's still alive. You're thinking of what's-her-name... Dian Fossey. *Gorillas in the Mist*. But the gorillas didn't kill her! It was poachers. Maybe the poachers tried to make it look like monkeys did it, but people don't believe it."

"Poachers? Why would anyone hunt a monkey? People eat them?"

"I think for trophies, mostly."

William sniffed.

"So that's what you did this weekend? Watched that bear movie?"

"Yeah. Well, I almost was going to see *King Kong*, but I didn't."

"*King Kong*. You know, the natives of Skull Island were more active in the old one. They would go, 'Ug a wug booga wooga *Kong*!'"

"In the old movie, there was this Chinaman on the boat, he was a member of the crew. And when the natives slip on the boat and kidnap the girl, one of them accidentally drops their beads. They had this Chinaman character find the beads on the ground and he goes, '*Craay-zee black men here!*' Ha ha ha ha! Later they had to cut that part out because they thought it was offensive to black people, having that Chinaman talking about the 'craay-zee black man!' Ha!

"You ever see that Steven Seagal movie where he's going after that guy, he turned out to be twins?"

"I'm not sure...."

"He's going after this Jamaican guy," William continued, "nobody can figure out why you can't kill him; and it turns out it's because he's got a twin. They don't tell you that at first."

"Yeah yeah; that was *Marked for Death*. I saw that when it came out."

"Well, there's one part where somebody puts a gun right

in this Jamaican guy's face—it might even be Steven Seagal who does it. Steven Seagal's got his gun up on him, and the guy goes, 'Keep a *cool* head, mon!' Ha ha ha ha! I got this friend, that's his favorite part in the whole movie. Every time we'd see each other, he'd say, 'Keep a *cool* head, mon!' and I'd say, '...Or you gonna see a *craay-zee* black man!' Ha ha ha ha!"

"So you already saw the new *King Kong*?"

"Not yet. When I took my girl to see *The Chronicles of Narnia*, I told her I would just as soon wait and go see *King Kong*, 'cause that started twenty minutes later. But she wanted to see the *Narnia*."

"I'll see it, even if it's bad. I'm a sucker for pretty much anything with big monsters fighting in it."

"In this new version they say they make him act more like a person; in the old one, he's like a brutal animal. I saw the preview, and they have him looking like a big spider monkey." He frowned, squinting a little as he chewed it over.

"I don't know," he said finally. "King Kong looks a little too monkeyish."

weighing the balls

IT WAS a cool morning for July, or at least cooler than we'd suffered through in the weeks before. But as William pulled the 842 away from the curb at Melrose, talk about the weather wasn't what was on his mind.

"Did you see somebody finally won the Mega Jackpot last night?" he asked me.

I hadn't.

"A hundred and seventy million," he said. "But now they made it even harder, 'cause there's so many numbers you have to pick. There's less chance someone's gonna pick all five numbers *and* the Mega."

"That's a lot of numbers to get right."

"Yeah. Too many. Usually I don't mess with it. I played a few times when it first jumped, you know, but I don't trust it. When that much money and that many people is

LUCKY WINNER OF CALIF.
ONE HUNDRED SEVENTY MILLION and NO/100
$170,000,000
JACKPOT
DOLLARS
MEGA
BALLS
Jackpot
170 MiLLiON

involved, somebody who shouldn't be's taking some of it somewhere."

"That's the way it always is," I agreed.

"There was the one guy who fixed it before, years ago. He fixed the Powerball. He had it figured out what numbers were gonna come up by weighing the balls or something."

I had a fuzzy memory of what he was talking about, but I didn't remember the details.

"All that stuff is crooked," he continued. "Did you ever hear about the guy who went after the racetracks? He came up with a way to cash unclaimed tickets. You know, if their horse wins but they don't know it and they throw their ticket on the ground? It just gets swept up and thrown in the garbage. They call that a 'unclaimed ticket,' and there's a thousand of them. This guy had figured out how to tell which tickets were unclaimed, then he'd print up his own and get the money."

"So he was able to print fake tickets?"

"Sure. It's not that hard. It's not like printin' money."

I supposed it wasn't.

"But it took time. 'Cause even if it's not hard to do, there's still not enough time to get your machine set up to print the ticket right then. So he would go home and print them and bring them in later. And what are the odds that someone with the real ticket's gonna show up the same time as you to cash it in?"

"Is that what happened?" I asked.

"Naw. One of the people he was working with ended up talking too much. There was a weak link in the chain," he said ominously. "But they found all that out later. He had another scam; that's where he got caught.

"You know how people bet on races from all over the country—New York, Florida, San Diego? Well, he was a computer genius, and he figured out that since there was a time delay on the results from out of state races, he could get the results and place a bet in that little space of time; he knew who was gonna win before anyone else did, before they announced it. They got what you call 'nipped in the bud.'

"He got three of the big races, boom, boom, boom. Then on the last race, he bet on all the horses, so those other wins wouldn't seem so suspicious."

"How is that not suspicious?" I wondered.

"I don't know, but that's how they caught him. Betting on all the horses, that's what caught their eye. And they got him." He waved his hand dismissively. "It was more complicated than I'm telling it, 'cause there was a lot of computer terminology involved that I'm not familiar with.

"So he thought he was protecting himself with that last bet, but that was the thing that put him away?"

"Um hm," he said. "If he hadn't been trying so hard to cover his ass, he'd be a free man."

the voice of reason

IT WAS Thursday morning, and I was the only one at the stop as William pulled the bus to the curb at Melrose. Even the 842 was practically empty.

"Where is everybody?"

"I guess they got the holiday off," William said.

"What holiday?"

"Isn't today a Jewish holiday?"

I didn't know. The 7:20 run of the 842 was generally day laborers and domestic help, and I hadn't given much thought as to who kept kosher.

"Yeah, see?" he said as we drove on.

"What?"

"Ha! See how they make them walk *behind* them? The women?" he chuckled, indicating a pair of pedestrians we'd passed too quickly for me to notice.

"Who?"

"You didn't see them, that couple there walking by? They must be on their way to services. They was both dressed all in white; he was wearing a *hammaka*."

The doors hissed, squealed and swung open, and we were joined by a frail looking woman in her late 60s. She was petite in a white ployester tracksuit and wide-brimmed straw hat. Her upper lip was glossy where her runny nose had gone untended.

She moved to open her purse, then thought better of it.

Leaning in to address William, she adopted a tentatively conspiratorial expression, warming up to say he just wouldn't *believe* what she was about to tell him.

"Oh!" she began. "I don't have..."

"You don't have your pass," he said, cutting her off. "You never have a pass. Six months now you been telling me you're gonna get a pass!"

"I know, I need to... I don't have it with me today, but..."

"You tell me that every time, and I *still* never seen a pass." William shook his head and threw the bus into gear, forcing her to grab a rail to steady herself.

"I just need to go to Wilshire and La Brea," she said.

Wilshire and La Brea was three miles and two turns in the wrong direction, and the 842 didn't go anywhere near there, coming or going.

"Right here, Wilshire and La Brea," she said as he pulled up to Santa Monica and Crescent Heights.

"She never has a pass," William explained to me, talking over her. "If they get on and just say, 'Can I ride?' I always say okay." He raised his voice in her direction. "But not *every day!*"

The door wheezed loudly and squeaked open. The woman made her way delicately down the stairs to the curb, exactly one stop from where she got on; she'd only traveled about three blocks.

"Next time, have a pass," he called after her. "This bus is the eight-four-two, not the eight-four-FREE!"

"I WAS on my way back yesterday and I remembered one I wanted to ask you if you'd seen," William said. "Did you ever see the one where Spanky is real little, and his parents make him sleep in his own bed instead of with them?"

"I'm not sure," I said. "What happens in it?"

"It starts out, his father says, 'The boy needs to sleep in his own bed!' So Spanky's in bed, but he keeps calling out to his parents: 'Can I have a drink of water? Can I this, can I that,' 'til it's like The Boy Who Cried Wolf. Then a burglar comes through the window! Spanky calls for his parents, but they don't believe him since he's been calling them all night. Spanky's going, 'There's somebody in here!'

"His father says, 'Oh yeah? Ask him his name,' and

the burglar says he's *Santa Claus!* Spanky says, 'It's
Santa Claus. And he's putting things in the bag!' His father
tells him, 'Oh, well make sure he knows where the good
silver is.' So he's *stealing* everything!

"Then Stymie comes up and he's got Petey the dog
with him. Spanky says, 'Santa Claus is here!' But Stymie
looks at him and he goes, 'That's not Santa Claus—that's
a *burglar!* Sic 'em, Petey!'" William laughed. "Ha ha ha!
'Sic 'em, Petey!' I liked Stymie. They would be doing crazy
things, but Stymie was always the voice of reason."

"Hey, did you see one," I started to ask, "where they had
a talent show, and a kid was playing the trumpet...."

"And the kids was eating lemons? Yeah, I saw that one."

"The one kid says to the other, 'You want a lemon? It's
good for your freckles!' I remember when we were little, me
and my brothers thought that was the funniest thing in the
world," I told him. "The kid was eating a lemon like it was
an orange!"

"Lemons is eatable!" he insisted. "It's something you
used to see more people do years ago. Young girls would eat
lemons with a peppermint stick in 'em."

"You know what," I said, giving it some thought, "now
that you mention it, I *do* remember seeing that... But years
and years ago, at a fair or something. I think I might have
even had one!"

"When I was growing up, we had a lemon tree in our
backyard," he told me. "We had a lemon tree, an avocado
tree and two peach trees. They would grow big. And you
know what happened to them?"

"What?"

"My dad cut 'em down."

"Really? Why?"

"None of us kids wanted to rake up the leaves! I used
to always be up in trees, growing up. That's not even
something kids today mess with, climbing up trees."

"Not so much around here."

"There was one tree in the neighborhood.... I was with
my little sister and I said, 'You wait here.' I climbed up
that tree, and the man who lived there came outside and
pulled me right down. He was a great big black man, and he
looked *mean.* 'Boy,' he said to me, 'If I catch you up in that

tree again, I'm gonna *kill* you!' I was scared!

"So I got my little sister and we went off to the park. Then on the way home, I said to her, 'You wait here,' and I went right back up it! I'm up there again—same tree!" He laughed.

"What, like a few minutes later?"

"Naw, this was hours later. We were playing at the park all day."

"Why would you do it again?!"

"I don't know why, exactly. Loose screw, I guess!" He laughed again. "Then I hear BOMP BOMP BOMP BOMP! It was the guy, coming out of the house and down the back stairs, coming after me!

He had a big cigar sticking out of his mouth and it was like a smokestack, little clouds puffing out... I was down from that tree and over that fence so fast! I grabbed my sister's hand and we took off out of there, but he chased us! Me and my sister, we were running and running... Look, he even got on a *bi*-cycle!" he roared, stretching out the word. "Dude was *on* me!" He laughed so hard at the memory, he was gasping.

"...On a *bicycle*! My little sister, she was maybe seven, I was probably nine." He sighed. "This was all after my father cut down our trees."

"I bet it smelled nice when you had them though."

"What did?"

"The lemon tree. They always have that great smell."

"I don't know, I actually don't remember ever smelling it. I was a kid, I wasn't real interested in lemons." He adjusted his cap. "We took 'em for granted. But I wish he hadn't cut down that avocado tree. I *like* avocados, now."

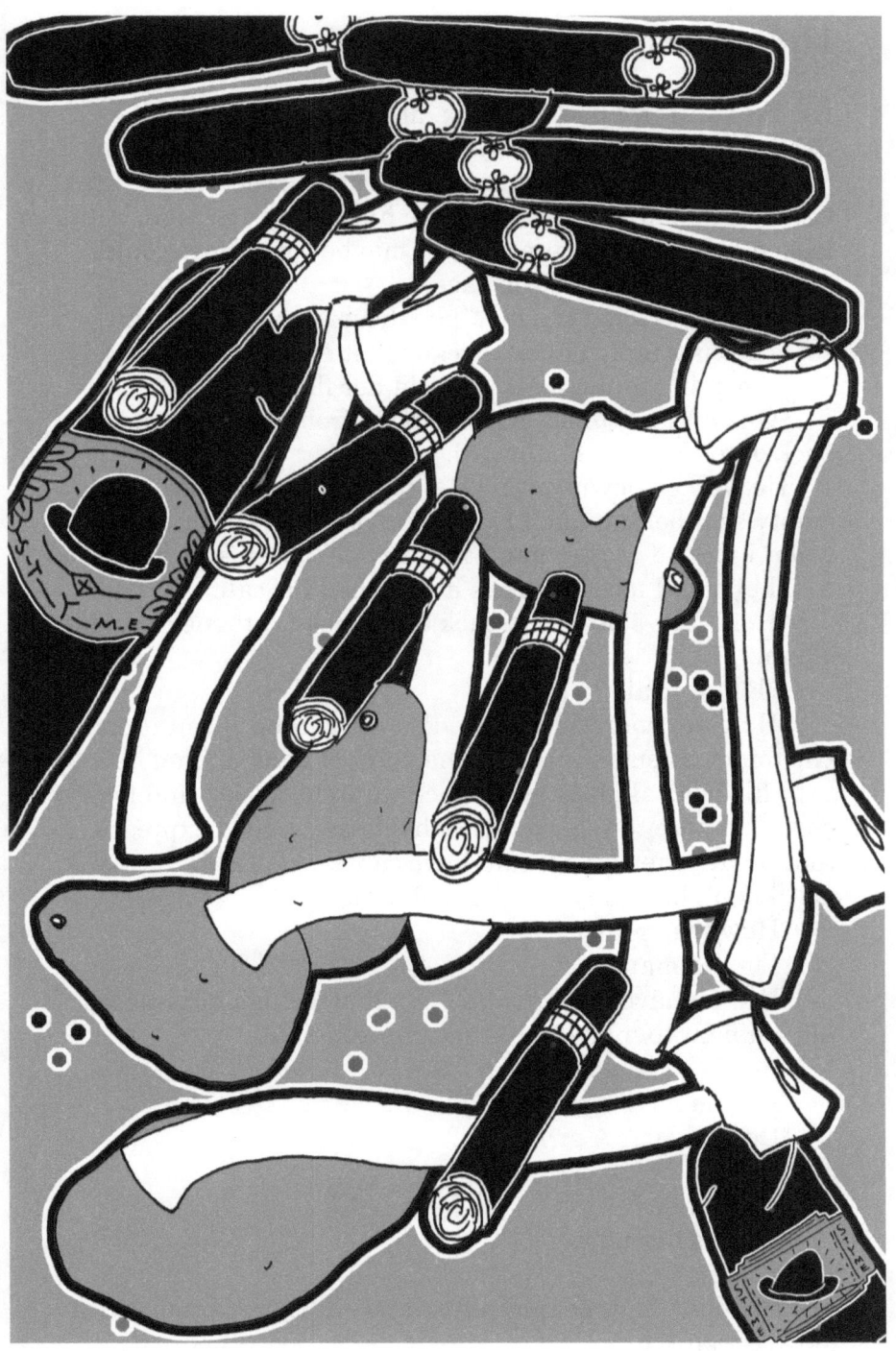

the great pumpkin

HE WAS short, round and black, and he carried himself
uncertainly onto the bus with a loping gait, displaying his
pass to the driver. With his belly straining the tight T-shirt
tucked into faded khakis he wore hitched up too high, he
looked able to dress himself, but maybe sometimes could
still use help with the shoelaces.

"You just riding all day?" the driver asked him with
some amusement. They'd already met earlier that morning.

"I'm going to the mall," he told her flatly.

"Okay," she smiled, pulling away from the curb and
back onto Ventura Boulevard.

He walked down the aisle a little stiffly and took the
empty seat behind me. I heard him ask a question, but
when I turned to respond, I realized he'd been speaking into
a cell phone. I faced front as he finished his call.

"Hello," he said to the back of my head. I turned around
again.

"Hello," I said to him.

"How are your kids?" he asked me without hesitation.
His tone was emotionless to the point of clinical, and he
kept his head slightly tilted back when he spoke, and looked
down his nose to regard me with a heavy-lidded expression
that on anyone else I would have called skeptical.

"I don't have any kids," I told him.

"How's your wife?"

"I'm not married."

"Do you have a *gwifwund*?" He had enough of a speech
impediment to make the word unintelligible.

"A—?"

"Do you have a gwifwund?"

"Do I have...? A girlfriend?

"Yeah."

"Yeah, I do."

"What's her name?"

"Sandee."

"Sandee," he repeated softly, and sat there a moment,
letting it sink in.

"So what are you up to today?" I asked him.

"I don't have anything to do all day," he said.

"Lucky you," I said. He didn't appear to see it as especially lucky.

"I'm going to the mall," he told me.

"Sure, why not," I shrugged.

"I live in a group home," he explained. "I don't like to stay around and do nothing all day. Maybe my brother will meet me there. He said he would. Either there or at the end of the line."

"And you'll go to the mall with him?"

"Yeah."

"That's a nice way to spend your day, with your brother." I meant it. I couldn't remember the last time I spent a day with either of my brothers. "But isn't the mall back that way?"

"That's a different mall," he said. "To get to this mall, you have to take the 166 bus."

"Okay. I've never been on the 166."

"Yeah. Are you going to work?"

"Yeah, I'm going to work."

"Where do you work?"

"Up the road, at a computer company."

"I'm not allowed to work yet. How old are you?"

"Thirty-four. How old are you?"

"Forty-two." He frowned.

"You don't look it," I told him. "You look younger." He did.

"I wish I was younger," he said. "Hey, do you have a dollar, or two dollars?"

"I don't," I lied. I had exactly two dollars in my pocket.

"That's okay," he told me.

We stopped at a red light. Through the window we had a clear view of a fenced lot on the corner. It was filled with pumpkins of every size and shape, displayed for sale on piles of loose straw and bales of hay. In the middle of the lot, they'd parked a tractor, stationing a hay-stuffed pumpkinhead scarecrow in denim overalls behind the wheel.

"They've got the pumpkins out," I said. "Pretty soon it'll be Christmas trees."

"Yes," he agreed.

We went a block or two without talking before he spoke again.

"Who are you gonna bring to the pumpkin patch?" he asked, matter-of-factly.

"To the pumpkin patch? I'd take Sandee."

"That's your gwifwund?"

"Yup."

He seemed satisfied with that.

my name is joe

"I COME here from Ecuador and I worked at the airport for nineteen years. Nineteen years from 1977 to 1996, and then they lay me off. Then in 1997 I get this job, driving buses. When I start, I know nothing about buses. But I learned.

"I make as much money now, after eight years, as I did in 1986 at my old job at the airport."

"So you've really been climbing your way back up to where you'd been."

"Yes, I had to start all over again."

"Where do you usually drive?"

"Downtown. I drive one of those big orange buses, sometimes three hundred people."

"That's a lot of people."

"It *is* a lot of people. When you have more people, it's more responsibility. But that means more money! You get maybe two dollars more an hour. I go where there's the most money."

"How many rotations do you do on that every day?"

"It's two and a half hours, that's the loop. I make three loops in a day, some days more. I work Monday through Thursday and that's my forty hours. So when they ask me to drive the 842 on a Friday, I say sure! It's all overtime for me."

"Do you like this run?"

"Sure. Sherman Oaks is nice. Ventura is nice. Very different from downtown."

"Not so nice?"

"Some of it, no. You get all kind of people. People who

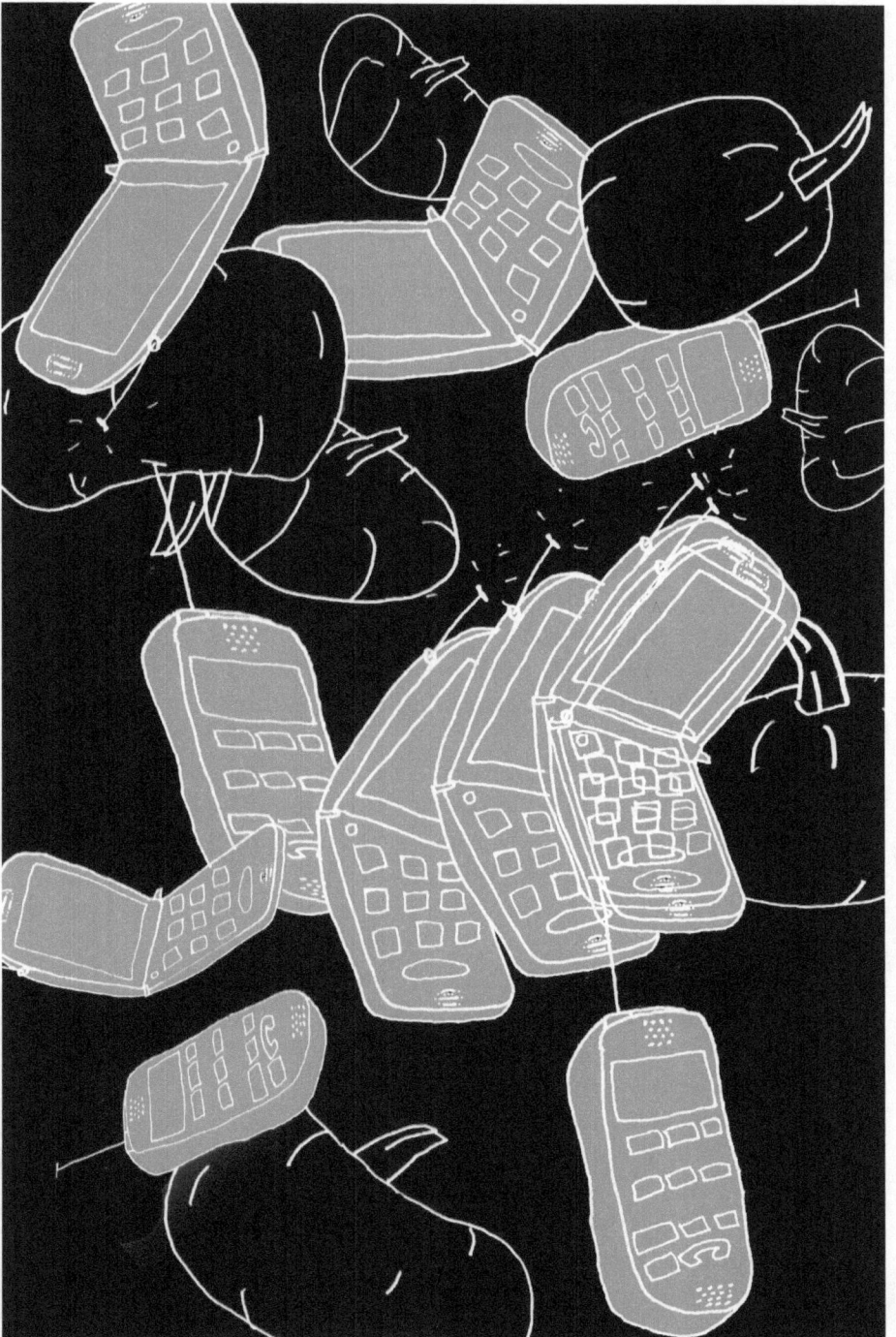

live on the street… You know, you get lots of crazy people. And kids, too. Kids like to—" He made a mouth with his hand, snapping it like a dog.

"They get in your face."

"Then they want to drink on your bus…" He shook his head. "I used to drive one of the big buses in a bad area, on King and Western. But the people there…" He put out a hand and rocked it from side to side. "Sometimes they get on and they seem all right, but then…

"One time this Muslim guy, he was praying on the bus— but not quietly. He was very loud. He even start singing!

"Next to him, he have this American guy. He have out his computer, he tap-tap-tap, working on his assignment. And then the Muslim guy start singing—loud! The American guy say, 'Please sir, can you keep it down?'

"He didn't like that! He say, 'Just because you are American, you can talk to me like that???' The American guy say, 'You are sitting close to me and being very loud.' You know, there's thirty, forty…there's a lot of people on the bus, you can't act like it's only your bus! But that guy, he say he's prejudiced. I tell him no, you're wrong." He frowned. "Things like that. Sometimes people are not very nice.

"People say when you too nice, it's not good. But I believe that if you give out a positive energy"—he pronounced the g as a y—"guess what come back to you? Positive energy! I was a salesman for five years, as a side job. And I saw that if you smile at someone, they smile back at you.

"This is me," I told him as we reached my stop. "Good talking with you. What's your name?"

He gave me a little wave. "My name is Joe."

"Glad to meet you, Joe."

"Glad to meet you."

I stepped down to the curb.

"It's Friday, it's a beautiful day," he said, looking through the windshield at the road ahead. "It feels like everything is gonna be easy today."

He closed the door of the bus and drove off.

MONDAY, William was back behind the wheel.

"What happened to you Friday?" I asked him. "I thought they might have switched your schedule on you."

"Nah. I was home, sick. Who drove the bus? Was it a woman, a black woman?"

"No, it was a guy. His name was Joe?"

"A Hispanic guy?"

"Yeah."

"Yeah, that's Joe. I've known him for a long time." He chuckled. "I'll tell you a story about Joe. This is funny.

"The first time he filled in on this line, he didn't really know this area. And he tells me he picked up this one passenger, and she sat in the back seat—" He paused cautiously, taking inventory of the passengers in the rearview mirror. When he saw it was only me and two other men, he continued.

"He says, it was unbelievable, this lady was sitting there with her legs wide open! He said he couldn't stop looking, and she didn't even notice. She just looked out the window the whole time with her legs spread. He said, 'William, she had the biggest, fattest thing I ever seen!'

"So I asked him, where did you pick her up? What stop was she at? He said Santa Monica and Harper. I said, 'Santa Monica and *Harper*? That's in West Hollywood!' He didn't know about West Hollywood.

"I told him, 'Joe, that wasn't no pussy! That was *nuts!*'"

sergio di nargerac

"DID you see the tribute on TV the other night, for Steve Martin?" William asked me as he drove.

"Nope. Was it good?"

"They were showing some funny clips of him. They had that one where he has the long nose.... What's the name of that movie?"

"*Roxanne*."

"*Roxanne*? Yeah, that's a funny movie. I saw the old version of that same story when I was a kid, about what's his name, Sergio Di Nargerac? I liked that one too."

"With José Ferrer?"

"I don't remember who was in it, but it was pretty good. You know who had a nose like that, in real life?"

"Who?"

"Patti LaBelle. When she was younger. She had a long nose just like that; it was like a witch! But she got a nose job or something."

"I don't know, I always really liked Steve Martin, but I don't like his movies so much now," I said. "Him and all those old *Saturday Night Live* guys, they all started out wild and funny, but now they're always playing it straight and letting crazy things happen to them. I'm not sure what that's all about. But I liked them all better when they were just funny themselves."

"What about that *Father of the Bride* movie?"

"Nope. He was pretty much the straight man in that, too." William was dismissive.

"Well, you can't be a buffoon *forever!*"

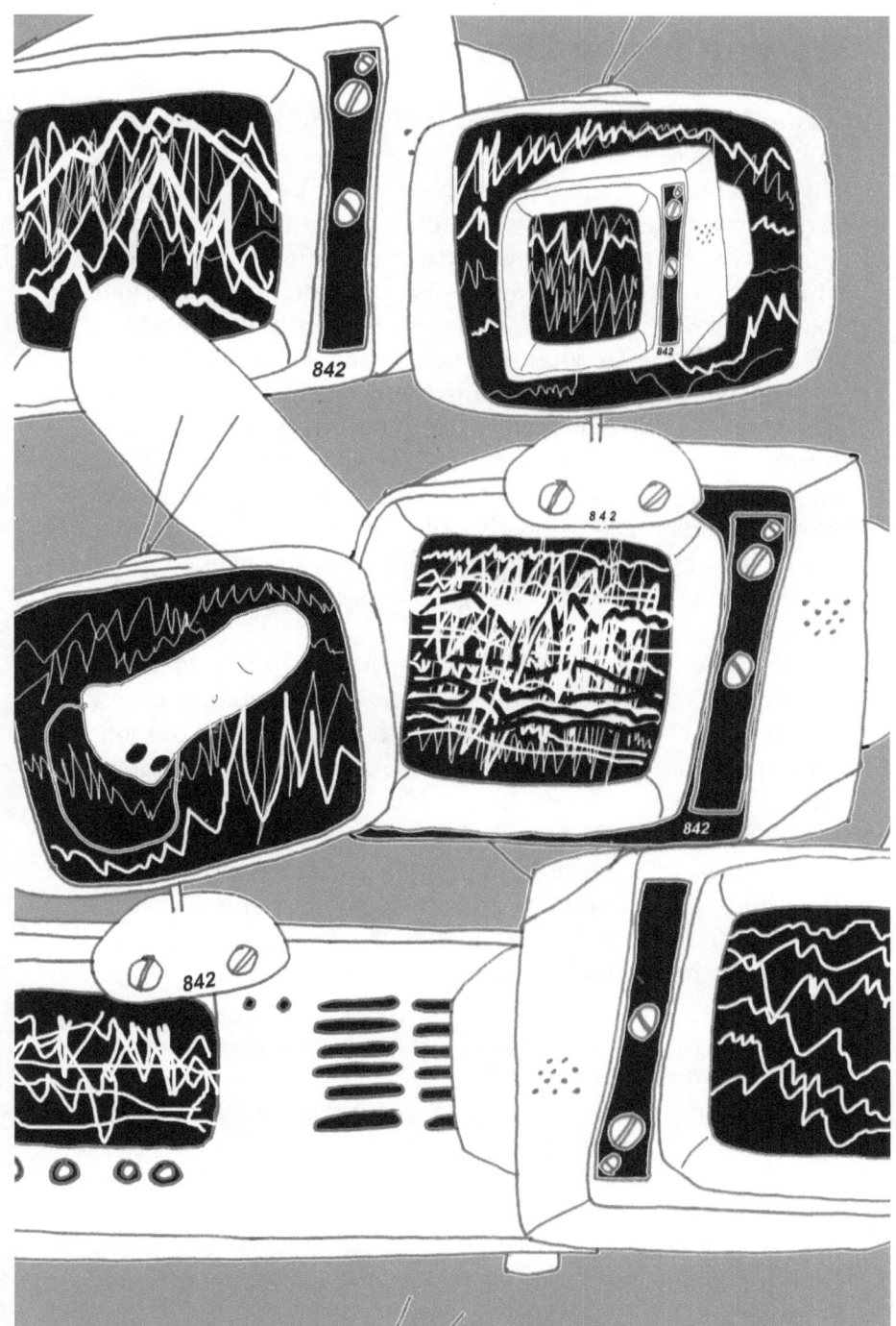

do you know this man?

JUST off Hollywood Boulevard at Highland is where I catch
my last bus to work every morning. There's an alcove in
the west face of the building there, and like the rest of the
structure, it's grimy and has gone unused for some time.

That's where a chubby white man with a wild afro of
brown curls had set up camp, just him and a pair of trash
bags, brown slouching blobs set on the stained concrete at
his feet, filled with whatever he'd found worth keeping.

He was missing most of his teeth but had managed to
hang on to the lower canines, and with his pudgy face and
round, wide eyes, he looked like a friendly bulldog fallen
on hard times. He had a gentle, spacey nature, and he sat
cross-legged on the sidewalk, a low-rent dirty Buddha in old
jeans, his sky-blue sweatjacket zipped to the neck.

"Can you spare any change? For a cup of coffee?" he
asked me.

"No. Sorry, man." Payday was coming, but it wasn't for
a few days and I was broke, with maybe ten dollars in my
pocket to see me through to the end of the week. I passed
him by to find a spot near the curb, one with a clear view
down the block to watch for my bus.

"'Scuse me, sir," he called out. "Do you know this man?"

I turned to see him holding up a piece of newspaper.
He'd folded it to display a picture accompanying an article
about preparations for the Academy Awards. One of the
figures in the photograph was unmistakable.

"That's you!" I said.

"Yes it is," he confirmed, pleased I'd recognized him so
easily. "I was in the paper."

Deciding that was somehow worth a dollar, I gave him
one. He was appreciative.

"Here," he said, holding the paper out to me. "Read what
it says."

I took it from him. The paper couldn't have been more
than a few days old, but already it was scuffed, as if it had
been scraped on the rough concrete.

In the picture's foreground, an older man in glasses

wore a dark, polyester blazer that identified him as part of
the security firm hired to oversee operations. But he was
not an especially imposing figure, and looked more like
a disgruntled old sportscaster. He frowned at the curly-
headed interloper (identified in the caption as "Theron
Tyler, a homeless man") standing knock-kneed on the heavy
red carpet unfurled on the sidewalk. Trash bags slung over
his shoulder like a sailor on leave, his arm was outstretched
and his face turned up to the sky with a dopey grin. He
looked every bit the happy hobo.

"They took that picture of me right on Hollywood
Boulevard," he told me proudly. "People saw me all over the
world!"

"Theron Tyler?" I asked, reading it *Thee*-ron. "That's you?"

"*Theron*," he corrected me, pronouncing it like *heron*.
"That's me all right."

"Theron," I repeated, handing him back the clipping. "I
can hear you've got an accent. Are you from the South?"

"Yes I am," he said, grinning big, empty gums.
"Arkansas."

"Arkansas! What brought you here from Arkansas?"

"Oh, I came out for the weather," he said. I told him I
guessed most people did.

All at once a thin man in a baggy leather bomber
jacket and bandana pulled up close at my side and swung
smoothly into position directly in front of me. Oozing cool
confidence, he greeted me as though we were old friends.
Tall and lanky, his light brown face was calm and open,
despite eyes that were slightly dazed.

"Hey man! It's good to see you, my brother!" he effused.
I didn't know him, but he clasped my hand in a warm soul
shake and pulled me close in a partial embrace. It was
eight in the morning and you could smell the booze when he
spoke, but neither seemed reason enough to refuse a little
easy brotherhood. He was clean, and he carried himself
well enough to maybe pass for someone who didn't live on
the street. We broke the hug and he stood at an odd angle,
bowed but solid, a dandelion in the summer breeze.

Theron made a move to reclaim the hijacked
conversation, but he was cut off.

"Man, you ain't got no teeth and I can't understand a

word you're saying. You probably already drunk."

Theron frowned. They knew each other, and the other man's attitude was less hostile than it was hierarchical; Theron was simply beneath his notice.

"Hang on now," I interjected. "You gotta give it to him. He did make the paper."

"Yeah!" Theron said. "Look!" He held out the clipping proudly. The other man took it and looked it over.

"People saw me all over the world," Theron insisted.

The other man sniffed, unimpressed. "And you carrying around the same dirty garbage bags, ain't you? Damn!"

"At least I'm in the newspaper," he boasted.

"Man, I like to stay *out* of the paper," the tall man retorted, never missing a beat. He handed the clipping back with disdain, returning his attention to me. "Hey, let me ask you something."

"Sure."

"You got anything you can give me to help a brother out?"

He may as well have been someone at the office asking if I could spot him a buck for the soda machine. A consummate pro, he operated on the presumption we both already knew I was going to give him the money; it was like he wasn't even asking. A real Mr. Clean. He should have had a bank of phones somewhere, pulling down real money.

As I dug for a dollar, I noticed something I hadn't before: he wasn't traveling alone. His partner stood off to the side, keeping close to the street. He was a frightened-looking brother, smaller, darker and dirtier than his friend. His clothes were ratty, and he had wild eyes, bumpy skin and chronic shakes. He was worse off than even sloppy, toothless Theron, since that much spooky was bad mojo for donations. Everything that made him most in need of a hand would be intimidating enough to prevent anyone from offering. It was his friend's gift for show business keeping them both afloat, and he maintained a safe distance while his partner worked so as not to queer the deal.

I watched him flinch as the 156 to North Hollywood heaved to a stop alongside the curb behind him.

"Listen," I said, nodding to the bus, "that's my ride. I'll have to catch you later. You guys take care of yourselves."

"All right all right. Thank you, my brother," the tall man

said, walking backwards down the block as his nervous
friend scuttled after him.

"I got a dollar!" the tall man shouted, a final jab at
Theron.

"Bye!" Theron said to me, refusing to acknowledge the
other man's taunts.

I moved to board with the rest of the riders. Behind me,
Theron tried to get the attention of a businesswoman as she
hurried past the alcove on her way to work.

"'Scuse me, lady," he called to her. "Do you know this
man?"

drive my car

"My girl needed a car to get to work; she been taking the bus every day. I knew my neighbor, he had bought a car for his wife, but she was real sick and she died. She never even got to drive it hardly at all. This car's just been sittin' for three years, he had it under a cover. Runs like a clock, and it's clean. I said, how much you want for that? He said fifteen hundred. I said naw, that's all right."

We hit a pothole, and William adjusted the bus' rearview mirror.

"I told my mother, ask him how much he want for that car, 'cause he can be a little strange, but he likes her. He told her twelve hundred; I said okay. I knew it was all right, so I bought it. I paid a hundred and fourteen dollars to get it registered, then I drove it straight to my insurance company and got it put on my insurance for another hundred and two dollars. Now all I got to do is take it in for smog and then go to the DMV."

"You're not wasting any time," I said.

"Yeah," he agreed. "It's a stick shift, though. So I'm gonna give my wife my old car and I'm gonna drive this one."

"Sounds like a good deal for everybody."

"It is! But then last night she says, 'I don't want that car.' I said, all the money I just spent? You crazy?"

"What brought this on?"

"Aw, you know," he started to explain. "Sometimes you get in little spats...."

"No, I mean, she said she wanted a car? Before?"

"Yeah, 'cause she been taking the bus to get to work every day."

"And now she doesn't want one?"

"She wants some car from a *dealership*. But you get a car from a dealership, you got a four-year note, maybe they try to get you for five. I had that before. I don't want no payment plan, and I know this car is good. She ain't never owned a car. I told her, my car is a fine first car for you! I said, you ain't had no car before; first time you go out, you gonna have a little ding here, a little ding there—that's why you need an old car!

"But she don't understand. Like when I found that diamond ring at the laundromat."

He pointed out the window.

"Look at that little baby with a cell phone!"

On the corner, an infant in a three-wheeled stroller studied the keypad of a flip-phone intently, using both tiny hands to hold it. Behind the stroller, a pair of young modern parents in workout clothes jogged in place as they waited for the light to change.

"He already know how to use it, too," William sniffed.

"Hang on," I said. "You found a diamond ring at the laundromat?!"

"Yeah, a few months ago. I didn't tell you about that? I was carrying my clothes back to my car and I saw something shiny on the ground. I picked it up, and it turned out it to be a diamond ring, just laying there in the parking lot.

"I tried to give it to her, to my girl, but she didn't want it, said she didn't like the style. I already bought her two other ones," he added.

"I told her, those are diamonds! You don't like it, you can have it broken down and made into something else." He shook his head.

"She didn't want to hear it. I took it to my mother, she said, 'Ooh, I like that!' She wanted to trade me for this diamond ring she had, see if my girl liked that one better. This is it, here."

He reached into his collar and pulled out a gold rope chain from around his neck. He slid the ring that hung from it around to show me before dropping it back inside his shirt.

"I don't know what she's thinking. Where she come from, they're poor—those people got nothing. It's a Third World country! That's the whole reason why she came here, to have a better life. I tell her, you think everyone in America is rich???

"She don't even tell her folks about me. And I took her to meet all *my* family right away! She says she can't tell them nothing about me unless I'm ready to fly them over here and set them up in America!

"So when she call and talk to them on the phone, she's

like—" He pressed a finger to his lips, then began to fume.

"I gotta be all quiet? In my own *home*?

"I said, you come to this country, meet a man, fall in love with him and get married, but I ain't good enough for them to know about me? What's *wrong* with me? Just because I don't have money to bring them over here and support them, too?" he bellowed, exploding all over again as he told the story. "I said, 'Eff you! *And* your family!'

"Next thing you know, she start packing her bags! Then I'm all, 'Now hang on there, baby...'" he laughed.

"Sounds like you're dealing with a little culture shock."

"That's exactly what I told her last night. It's cultural. I told her, around here in America, that's not the way we do it. When you get married, that comes first. You don't forget your family, you don't forget your mother and your father, but they are second to your husband or your wife—that's your immediate family. Am I right?"

"Her family is in Eastern Europe somewhere?"

"Have you ever heard of Georgia? That's where they are. Georgia, used to be in Russia."

"Okay."

"Talkin' you want me to feed them and support them," he muttered. "And you barely in the car *yourself*!"

He shook his head.

"Broads is crazy, man!"

driver's education

THE bus stop under the overpass wasn't my usual corner, but I'd walked a few blocks out of my way to hit the convenience store for cigarettes. Technically I was quit, but lately I'd been bumming off the guys I worked with at breaks. I didn't want a reputation as a mooch, so I figured to cover my tab buying a pack for them every few weeks. Standing near the curb, I helped myself while I waited for the bus.

Above me, the streetlamp flickered once then slowly faded to gray with a dull fizzing sound; behind the lens, the

filament was like an antique flashbulb dying off after the pop.

From the opposite corner, a thin man in his 60s trotted across the street in my direction. He was dressed casually in jeans, a golf shirt under a soft brown leather jacket cut big. An L.L. Bean ball cap hid most of his short white hair, and a frost-colored biker moustache stood out against his dark complexion, helping to camouflage the softening of his chin.

"Lousy time for the light to go," I said after a bit.

He looked warily to the darkened streetlamp, then back down to me, making up his mind.

"This is a hard corner to see you on already," he agreed at last. "You see the bus coming, you have to jump out in front of it and wave your arms, you want it to pick you up. This time a night, they'll drive right past you. I used to drive buses, there were a lot of times I did that myself. I feel bad about it now."

He showed me the half-smoked stub of a cigarette in his fingers.

"Hey, I'm smoking shorts. Can I get one of those from you?"

I handed one over.

"Thanks, man." He lit up from a near-empty book of paper matches out of his jacket pocket.

"You drove for MTA? How long?"

"12 years! That was enough for me."

"Oh yeah? When was this?"

"A long time ago. I used to drive the 212 when it went all the way to Burbank airport!" He blew out a cloud of smoke. "This is when there was some crime on the buses. I mean *crime*. It was real bad. It's much better now. They have cameras and police radios…. When I was driving, we had a silent alarm, but even then it took 'em 45 minutes before they'd get there.

"You never knew who was gonna be on your bus. You got 5150s, drug heads, crazies. There was a lot of real crime. I been hijacked, assaulted, robbed, beaten up…." He lowered his voice, as if sharing a confidence. "Some of the lady drivers, they, uh, some of the lady drivers were raped…. There's some rough lines in Los Angeles."

"So how do they decide who drives where?"

"It's up to you. You can choose what line you want.

For instance, you make more money driving the busier lines, because of standing accidents. You got more people standing, they're more likely to get hurt.

"But there's lines drivers would refuse to take. Especially on late shifts. Because what happens is, the clubs'll close at 2 a.m., and then they'll get on the bus and keep it going there 'til the next day. Back there shooting dice, drinking. The whole night!

"Some drivers would carry a weapon to work. I never did that. I never carried a weapon."

"Let me ask you. I see signs on the buses saying if you see someone tagging up the bus, or if you notice suspicious behavior, tell the driver. What exactly do they expect the driver to do about it?"

"Listen, the bus company cares about one thing: keeping the buses rolling. You're being paid to drive that bus, not be the police.

"Hell, I've left with a brand new bus and come back with the whole bus covered in graffiti—on the *inside*. Not just magic marker, but scratched in, and spray paint... But the outside looked fine! Nothing you can do about it, and the bus company expects that anyway. Wear and tear.

"There's a lot of things you just have to get used to thinking about differently if you're going to be a bus driver. Like, when I first started driving, I used to wear a tie to work every day." His fingers went to his neck to straighten an invisible knot, and he smoothed a hand down its imaginary length. "A nice MTA tie. I took pride in myself.

"And my wife...my wife made sure I had every button shiny, looking all smooth. She'd send me off to work looking..." He fished for "immaculate" but didn't land it. "...She sent me off to work looking *explicit*.

"I'd be looking good, and I was always in a good mood. All the women riders would flirt with me, they'd be slipping me their numbers, up here," he grinned, patting his left shirt pocket. "But what I didn't realize was, watching the ladies make all that fuss over me was making Joe over there jealous. I didn't even see it.

"So they were kicking my ass. Putting guns to my head. And these are my own people! It was all new to me. I'd never lived in the 'hood; I came here from Kentucky!

West L.A. is where I lived.

"It was the experienced drivers who let me know what was up. They told me, 'You look too happy.' I was just being myself! But they said, 'That's all right, but you gotta keep that inside.' In some areas, people don't want to see somebody who's happy, who looks like they're doing well. They see you happy, they figure you got something good going on for yourself. Maybe they don't have what you have. They get jealous. And then they get mad.

"So you can't do that. You drive into Crenshaw, you take the tie off, and you unbutton that top button. Don't be laughing, all jolly. Try to look like you from the 'hood. Once I started doing that, I stopped having those kinds of problems.

"Now I worked with some pretty tough drivers. Guys who could handle themselves, and did...and I'm bringing them flowers in the hospital. They're all broken up. They can't work, so they can't pay their bills. End up losing their jobs, can't make love to their woman....

"What you learn is that it's nothing to do with being brave, or being cowardly or anything like that. It's that there are evil people in the world, people with nothing to lose. People who go out looking for some kind of trouble, because they just don't care about anything. Evil people! You got to try to stay away from the evil people if you can.

"When I was younger I didn't think like that, but I do now. Now, I know the most important thing is when I get home, my body is in the same condition as when I went out!

"Somebody's being rude, you gotta learn to ignore it. I was on the bus the other day, and this young guy was yelling about something, calling up at the driver, looking to start something. But the driver was smart." He pursed his lips and put a finger to them. "He didn't say anything."

"So no cowboys need apply?"

He shrugged.

"Maybe they do, but they don't last long. But even the guys who aren't like that have other things to worry about. Like if they take all the overtime they get offered, they end up stressed out, their health breaking down.... It's not good to work all the time. It's not healthy!

"That's what happened to me. I was working all the

time, grabbing every bit of overtime they'd give me; my shift was 12 ½ hours. I spent so much time working, I didn't even know my *dog*. But I felt like I had to, because by then I'd got used to it, and I'd started living beyond my means; you always figure you'll be able to catch up later. By the time I left, I was making $60,000 a year. And that was real good at that time. But I never got to be home, never got to spend time with my wife.

"Then my wife started working too, and I was finally able to cut back on my hours a little bit and have a normal life.

"The company... Once the company sees you'll go along with everything they want from you, they'll call you on your day off, see if you want to drive. And all that overtime money's too good to say no to. They'll work you 'til you're in your grave, then they'll step over that to get to the next guy coming. It's a company. It's a business. That's the way it is. Looking after yourself is your own responsibility."

He craned his neck up the block.

"Here it comes, finally." He nodded in the direction of the approaching bus.

As it slowed and pulled to the curb, I moved aside so he could board first. He waved me off.

"You're not riding?"

He shook his head no. "Hey, when you get on, ask him where's he been? They love that."

"Right," I said as the doors swung open.

He raised a hand in farewell as I climbed the stairs into the bus.

"Thanks for the smoke."

miss guy

"THAT'S a 1947 Packard!" William said as one passed us going the other way.

"Oh yeah?"

"Yeah. Those old cars, sometimes those doors didn't close right. You could fall out of them! I did. I fell out of a moving car one time. My mother was driving and I was standing on the seat. I tumbled right out and rolled into the gutter."

"What happened?"

"I picked myself up, looked around, and said, 'What's going on?' Ha!

"I knew this one guy," he went on, "he jumped out of a second story building and landed on his bare feet—and he kept on running! He showed up at my house. I asked him what happened to his shoes, and he told me the whole story.

"He was in his apartment and he hears a knock on the door. BAM BAM BAM! A *serious* knock. He peeks out the peephole and there's two men there, looking all gangsterish, topcoats and everything.

"He told me he knew it was something to do with his girl; she owed somebody money or something. They were in the process of breaking up at the time.

"He goes, 'Yeah?' They go, 'Is so-and-so in?' Asking for him by name. He figured his girl must have told them about him. He says, 'What 'chu want?' They say, 'We just want to holla at you a minute.'

"So he runs into the bedroom and drags the dresser over in front of the door. Then, BAM! He hears them break down the front door; they're calling out, 'So-and-so, where you at?!'

"He knew if they got through the front door, they'd get through the bedroom door no problem, even with a dresser across it. So he went out the window. Jumped out in his bare feet, right onto the concrete! But he was all right. You know, once that adrenaline gets going, you can do all kinds of things you didn't know you could do.

"He said he went back later to gather up some of his things. He talked to the manager, and the manager told him those two were straight-up gangsters!

"When he told me that story, I thought maybe they were after him, and he just didn't want to tell me about it, but then she ended up going to jail and he didn't, so I guess he was telling the truth.

"I said to him, 'It didn't occur to you instead of jumping, to just hang out the window and drop down?' He said, 'Uh uh. I went out *feet first*.' Ha!

"I fell out of the second floor of the building I grew up

in, too. When I was a baby. It was a two story building, and we lived upstairs. Somebody came to visit or something, and they left the back door open. I just crawled on out and fell. My parents didn't even realize I had wandered off. I was okay, though."

"So you fell down two flights of stairs?"

"We had stairs, but I didn't fall down the stairs; I went out the side."

"Did you land in some bushes or something?"

"Uh uh. On the *concrete*."

"But you were all right?"

"I was fine. God *protects* fools and babies!" he laughed.

"How did your family figure out what happened?"

"I don't know who discovered me. Probably one of my godparents, because after that my godfather told my mother, 'Well, you can't kill him!' See, they lived in a little house in the back. It was all split up so there was a bunch of people living there. My brother's godparents lived back there, too. They all shared a kitchen and a restroom, so they was close, you know?"

"Is this on your mother's side or your father's side?"

"Neither."

"They weren't blood relations?"

"Not blood relations, but we were all like family. They were my aunt and uncle. Yeah, I used to visit with them all the time. They took *care* of me at Christmas—cowboy outfit with a hat, a vest... *Two* guns in the gun belt! Ha! I loved my godparents. I still remember their old phone number, even though it's probably twenty years since I called it.

"My godmother didn't have to work. She would stay at home and watch *Queen for a Day*. You probably too young to remember that."

"Yeah, but I've heard about it."

"All these ladies'd tell their story and then they'd pick one of them, the one who had it the worst. They'd put a tiara on her head and wrap a cape around her, give her a *skepter*. Then she was Queen for a Day. The host was Jack... Jack somebody, I forget.

"My aunt, she passed away. But my uncle's still alive. I went to see him just last week, he turned ninety-four. I brought him a cake. He got this woman lives with him now, but he's still sharp. This one woman who came to live with him before her, two weeks after she move in, she says, 'I have to ask you something. Where you keep your...'" —he lowered his voice ominously—"'...*insurance papers?*' Ha! He didn't let her stay around too long after that!"

"And he lived in the house behind yours?"

"Back when I was growing up, yeah. This lady, Miss Guy, she owned the property, and at some point she made the building into a rooming house. She was a older lady, older than my mother. She was well-off. I don't know where she acquired her wealth from, but you didn't see a lot of black people with wealth in those days." He thought a moment. "Well, it wasn't that unusual, but it wasn't all that usual either! She lived downstairs and we lived upstairs. She was a invalid. I never remember her walking; maybe when I was a baby she could.

"She didn't have no children of her own; we was like her grandchildren. Sometimes my parents would go out and they'd say, 'Now you take care of Miss Guy. You listen for her if she needs something.' She had a little bell, and she'd ring it when she wanted to call us. She wasn't real demanding; mostly she'd just want us to roll her up real tight. She had one of those beds, you could turn a wheel on it so she could sit up or lay down.

"But sometimes she'd get the idea that she was gonna attempt to walk. She'd tell us, 'I think I can, today.' We'd say, 'Oh no, Miss Guy! You can't do that!' All scared."

"Why were you scared?"

"I guess we were worried she was gonna try to get up and fall down on the floor! We were so small, we couldn't have picked her up again if she did. Maybe when we was real little we saw that happen, I'm not sure.

"She was a real sweet lady. When she died, she willed that whole place to my brother, my sister and me. She made my parents the executors, so we stayed. Everybody else moved out, but we all stayed close.

"Her first name was Emma. You know anybody with that name? It used to be real popular for ladies, 'Emma.' You don't hear it so much anymore."

"Emma J. Guy," he said, drifting a little. "Yeah, I knew Miss Guy."

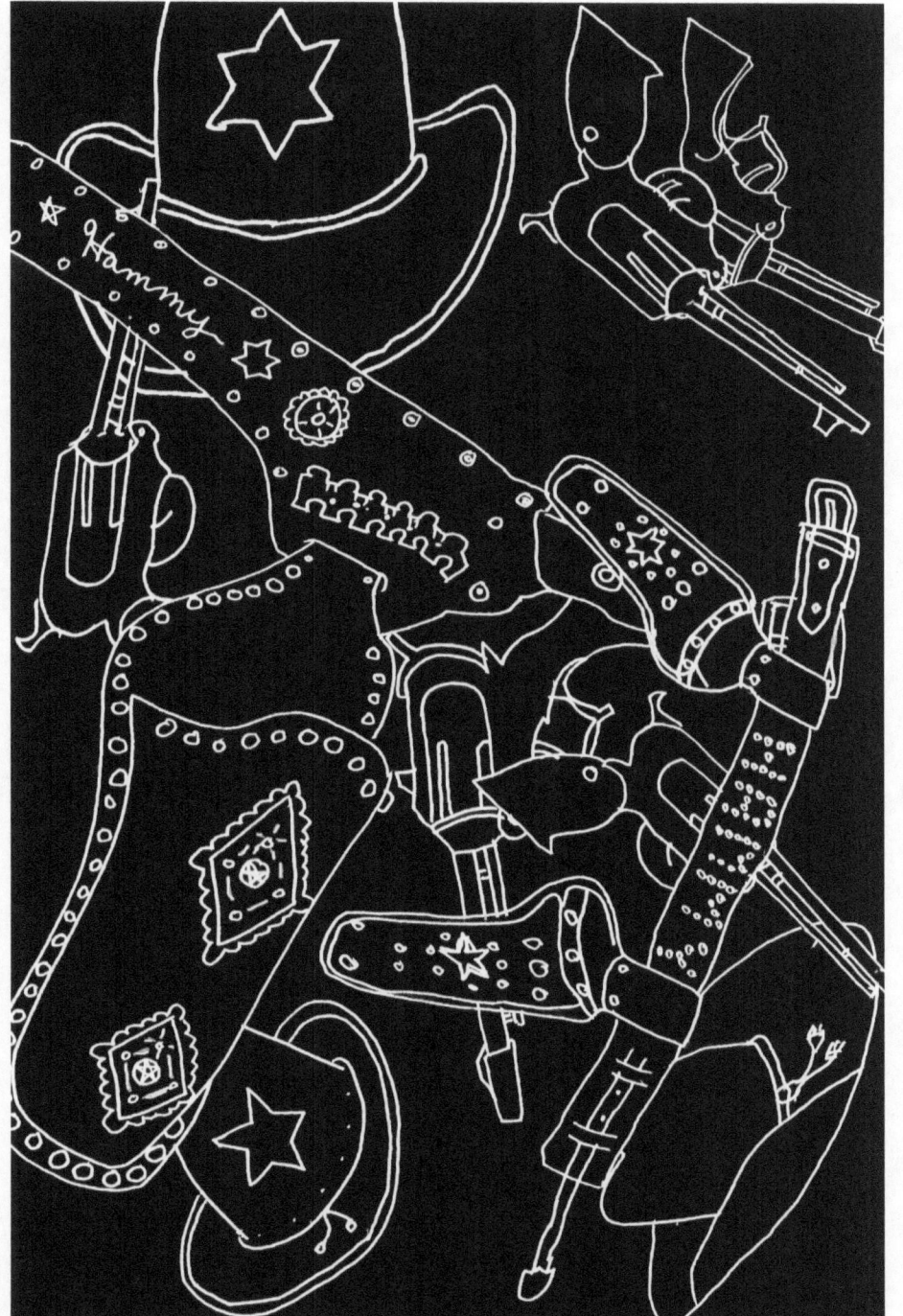

can't slow down

LIKE many of the little shops caught in the Bermuda Triangle of indefinable foreign otherness on Fairfax at Beverly, the small Russian drugstore near the corner was a place of business that bordered on an enigma. It was closed more than it was open, and had a firm policy of quiet hostility to outsiders—which I suppose was just about everyone. But it was close to home and they sold bus passes, so I was a monthly customer.

It was a place of bare, notched aluminum grocery shelves and a distinct feeling of under-the-table business no one would ever know the whole story on. A mood of general suspicion hung in the air, and it cut both ways; however curious you might be about what really went on there, the sour demeanor of the matronly blonde at the register was a constant reminder that, as far as they were concerned, you probably shouldn't even be there in the first place.

Basic upkeep had been an early casualty in the shop's war on customer service. Everything the sun could touch had blanched to illegibility, and the crinkled plastic sunshade hanging in the front window only managed to make everything look even older and dustier through its thin green tint.

If only the place held something—anything!—of the charm and mystery of an old apothecary: a few sagging shelves, some ancient remedies, even a single piece of exotic corked glassware labeled by hand.... But there was no adventure to be had in squat, white plastic bottles in uniform shapes with generic labels, scattered carelessly on the prefab shelves.

A press-letter board in the window of the tiny pharmacy station in the back listed hours of operation as Monday through Friday, with Saturday's schedule left blank. Wedged into the ribs of the sign at the bottom, black plastic characters spelled out the words CLOSED SUNDAY, but it was never really open. The shelves behind the service window were empty as those in the rest of the place, and the pharmacy lights were always out.

"Do you not fill prescriptions here?" I asked, purely out of curiosity. It was, after all, a drugstore.

"In thirty days," she said flatly. Her accent was thick; like her makeup, like her perfume.

When I came back for a new bus pass the following month, an accordion gate of heavy, dirty steel secured the storefront, and the inside was dark. But even this couldn't be taken as meaning anything for certain. They could be open again in a week, and no less displeased to see you. I saw the 217 approaching from down the block, and I crossed the street to catch it.

THE intersection was just off the freeway, and traffic there was as heavy and reckless as you might expect from the stretch of overpass leading to the Valley's primary escape hatch.

Most of the sign-carrying homeless who worked the local stoplights found the overpass too fast and too dangerous for business, and there were plenty of easier and more lucrative opportunities safely close by in either direction. But the lost-looking old man in faded olive drab didn't carry a sign, and he didn't even appear to see the angry traffic as he stood motionless on the corner, far too close to the edge of such a hazardous curb. With a camouflage trucker's cap and a vacant expression, he faced down some of the worst driving in town.

Unflinching, he stood unruffled and maybe even unaware of the eighteen tons of bus that roared past mere inches from his face. "LA DOLCE VITA," the loose cursive graffiti sprayed on his cap read. I hoped it was.

I SAT alone toward the back. The seat ahead of me was empty, and a woman with a short Jheri curl sat sidesaddle in the next seat down. She wore a fall coat too warm for the weather, its hood trimmed in thin faux fur. She chewed on her fingers and spat a piece of chipped nail at the window, then turned to me and smiled sheepishly.

"I'm a little nervous," she said. There was something familiar about her, but I couldn't quite place it. I noticed a small glob of what looked like chewed graham cracker on the shoulder of her coat.

"What's that about, do you think?" she asked, with a nod
out the window. I followed her eyes to a large movie poster
flour-pasted to the side of a construction site. It was an
unsettling image: an antiqued portrait of a young girl, with
only smooth, blank flesh where her mouth should've been.

"I don't know, but it looks like a horror movie," I said.

She laughed.

"When Do We Eat?" she read aloud, and I realized she
meant the poster *next* to that one. On that poster, a fat,
middle-aged man clutched his head with both hands, mouth
agape in a silent scream while a rogues' gallery of broad
Jewish stereotypes lined the dinner table behind him,
silverware clenched in their fists. In its way, it could also be
a horror movie.

"Hey," she said, turning around in her seat completely
to face me. She winked and smiled, and I noticed what
must have been another piece of graham cracker stuck
to the opposite cheek. Noticing her small, round eyes set
deep under her brow, I suddenly realized the person she
reminded me of was Samuel L. Jackson.

"It's my birthday today," she informed me, squeezing
lotion from a tube into her palm and rubbing her hands
together.

"Oh yeah?" I said.

"Hey," she called again, looking up from her hands.
She winked at me a second time and I smiled. She opened
her mouth and pushed out her small, pointed tongue.
She curled it lasciviously, lustfully, in my direction, then
switched abruptly to a demure, coquettish grin, batting her
lashes. The dramatic shift made me laugh out loud. She
didn't mind.

The bus stopped and she gathered her several shopping
bags, then rose to exit the rear doors. Before she left, she
grinned and wriggled the fingers of her free hand in a
delicate farewell.

"Happy birthday," I told her.

At the front, a broad-shouldered, big-bellied man in
deck shoes hobbled aboard, his pasty complexion lobster
red from alcohol and sleeping outdoors. Wearing flowered
blue swim trunks that strained at the seams, he moved
as if in physical discomfort. A too-small corduroy Oxford,

barely buttoned over a tummy-hugging polo shirt, topped
his ensemble, with both coming up short enough to leave
his sagging stomach exposed. It drooped over the stretched
elastic of the trunks' waistband as he stiffly shuffled down
the aisle.

There were plenty of seats, but he elected to remain
standing. Holding the top rail for support, he squeezed
his eyes closed, eased his head back, and broke into some
Lionel Richie at performance volume.

"And I'm ooon my waaay..." he sang to the ceiling.

lady bird

Bus fares had gone up again, and along with the higher
rates came the usual one-two punch of inconvenient
schedule changes and reduced service. The bus to work that
used to run every twenty minutes now came once an hour,
then some days it didn't come at all. And when it skipped
a run like that, everyone on the route was not only late
getting where they were going, but in a lousy mood when
they got there.

"They never fuck you *a little*," was how it was explained
to me by a guy at the stop. His name was Gutierrez, and he
was okay. Early 40s, black, bald. Not always a jacket-and-
tie man, but he paid attention to how he dressed. He liked
to put himself out there as a man on the move, and made
a point of shaking my hand each time we met. He worked
over the phone in boiler-room mortgage refinancing, and
the grave tone of his frequent shop talk made it plain that
making money was something that was important to him.
He did well for himself, to hear him tell it. But I wasn't
convinced when he said it was the money he saved on gas
that kept him on public transportation.

"I'm about ready to turn around and head home," he
announced as he scanned the horizon for the bus. It was
already late enough to probably not be coming. The next
day was a holiday, but this year it fell on a Wednesday,
leaving everyone feeling screwed out of a three-day

weekend—Gutierrez in particular.

"The thing is," he continued, "I've got two clients expecting calls from me today. But one of them's not 'til 6:30! I might just go in and get all their information, then leave. Do those calls from home."

"Yeah, but if you're gonna take a day, wouldn't you rather take the day after off, instead?" I asked.

"You're right about that," he said, weighing his options. "I might need to! You have to be careful with taking days off, though. This one lady I worked with? She was a former dope addict or something. She told people, I guess. But she was on her way; she was pulling down some big checks."

"I've worked sales with people in recovery before," I said. "They tend to be very motivated."

"Well, also they're used to *hustling*!" he chuckled gravely. "That's what it was with this lady, I'm pretty sure. She was at work last Monday and she said, 'I'm having an allergic reaction.' She showed everybody her arms, and you could see she was. She's out Tuesday, Wednesday, Thursday... But she never calls in. Then she comes in on Friday—we get paid every Friday—and she's like, 'Are the checks here yet?' They said, 'Where you been all week?' She said, 'Well, Tuesday I had to go to the hospital. Then Wednesday...'"

He frowned.

"It's terrible, and I'm not saying she's lying, but somebody from the office actually had seen her on Wednesday, and they saw her walking down Hollywood Boulevard, kissing up on her man. But she says, 'On Wednesday I was coming out of the hospital, and I was assaulted. These two men pulled me into an alley, and they raped me. I was raped.'" He raised his palms defensively. "Like I said, I'm not saying she's lying, but that other lady saw her...." He arched an eyebrow.

"I'm not sure where exactly your head would have to be, to be looking for an excuse and jump right to that," I said.

"She had a relapse or something," he assured me, waving off any uncertainty. "That's what it was. Anyway, they weren't having it. When she said that, they said, 'Well, what happened *Thursday*?'"

TELEVISION monitors had lately become standard equipment on city buses, one at the front and one in the rear. This ensured no one was spared the blare of low-rent advertising and inane short programming at those times of day when you least want to deal with either.

"Get-rich-quick schemes," Gutierrez said, nodding to the TV as he stood to exit. "That's all they run, all day on these things." On the screen, a stiffly computer-animated fox blinked dead, beady eyes from behind an executive's desk. Gesturing robotically, it extolled the importance of getting in early on property foreclosures.

ONCE we were into North Hollywood, the crowd thinned and I found an open seat near the rear door. I sat on the aisle, resting my bag on the seat by the window.

An elderly Asian woman boarded at the next stop. She looked frail at first glance, but when she walked she was limber and energetic, and moved with the weightless bounce of a marionette. Though it seemed to have been designed for a child, her matched outfit hung loose on her tiny frame. Somewhere between a fleece tracksuit and pyjamas, it was downy and pink except for a white patch on the front showing a cartoon of a zebra standing near an orange tree.

Her gray straw hair was cropped short in a severe, masculine style with one-inch bangs on her forehead. Her ears were framed by sharply sheared ninety-degree angles that left a broad expanse of bald, freckled skin on either side of her head. The look was almost Mayan.

She marched down the aisle, all scruffy determination, stopping at my seat to stare at me. Despite her size, she made for an arresting figure.

I took my bag in my lap and slid over to the window, offering her the open seat.

"Yes?" she asked.

"Please," I confirmed.

She twinkled in appreciation and turned to settle in. But rather than face front, she daintily set herself down sideways, legs in the aisle. Then she inched her tiny rear back bit by bit until she was pressed firmly to my side, shamelessly reclining as if I was the arm of a sofa. If she looked like a marionette, resting on me she felt like one, all balsa wood pieces and thin doll's clothes.

She turned to face me, her tiny features playfully defiant. Brown eyes glittered behind gentle triangles sculpted in the fair skin at her forehead. Her mouth was flat and abbreviated, a happy hyphen. She was old, but her skin was soft and unlined. Petite jowls weighted her delicate face as if to keep it from floating away.

I smiled at her cheeky personality, and her eyes lit up. Beaming, she brought her hands together in a silent, joyful clap. Crooking one foot under herself, she let the other leg dangle. Short enough that it hung several inches off the floor, she kicked and swung it freely with the rhythm of the ride.

A swarthy man near the front grinned as he watched us, entertained. To much of the bus, we were captivating stuff.

"She likes you, man," he said.

I shrugged.

"Miss," he called to her, "you can sit over here if you like. There's plenty of room here at the front." He indicated the several empty seats around him.

The lady looked up at me.

"I should move?" she wondered. Her English was halting but sweetly musical, and each syllable rang a little glass bell.

"You're welcome to stay," I said.

Her face bloomed and she nestled happily at my side. A moment later she stood up sharply and shivered like a duck shaking off water, then sat back down, once more cradled comfortably against me. She turned her face up to mine, her little doll's eyes beaming.

"You look like Elvis," she told me.

absolutely positively

HE WASN'T young, exactly, but he had the energy and enthusiasm of a younger man. You could see it in his eyes, and in the intensity of his sharp features.

His short brown afro was fashionably knotted, and he wore loose clothes in earth tones and natural fabrics.

He carried a half-size spiral notebook, each page filled with his own intense ballpoint. He was clean and tidy, but carried a strong and unusual scent; organic, yet somehow clinical. It was the aroma of people on the aggressive end of healthy lifestyle choices; apple vinegar, maybe. It wasn't unpleasant, but it was unique, somehow both strange and familiar, like the way real vitamin tablets smell, or used to smell when they came in brown glass bottles from small dusty shops run by aging beatniks. You give off what you put in, and probably to him, you, me and everyone else smelled of old cheese and rotting meat. I've heard that's what the Japanese think we smell like, though apparently they're too polite to mention it.

We were friendly enough to say hello and sometimes make small talk mornings while we waited together for the Rapid bus west on Ventura Boulevard. I didn't know his name, but not knowing someone's name is rarely an impediment to conversation—or even confidences—on public transportation.

The last time I saw him, the 842 over the hill had been delayed, and that cost us our connecting bus. We were waiting to catch a later Rapid, but I was certain I'd miss my next connection—my third and last bus, and one that ran far less frequently than the first two. Besides leaving me with almost an hour's wait for the next one, I'd also end up at least forty-five minutes late for work. It didn't even matter that the driver of that bus was generally at least ten minutes late, since as a rule, any time I was running behind, she was right on time. Or early.

"Pretty late today, huh?" I said to him.

"Yeah, it's five to eight now," he told me.

"Really? Ah, I'm screwed then."

"Why's that?"

I explained why as the Rapid pulled up and we boarded.

"Is your work close enough to walk to?" he asked as we took seats.

"I wish," I said. "It's about a twenty-five minute drive on the bus."

"That's not so bad!" he insisted. "So you're twenty minutes late for work. That's not a big deal." I didn't follow his math, but that was okay.

"At my job, I doubt they'll care anyway," I shrugged. My job or what anyone there might have to say about anything didn't set me off so much, and really, missing a bus is a small inconvenience. But the same way a sudden stop in an automobile jerks anything not stuck to the dashboard into your lap, sharp halts to personal momentum at the wrong time can stir up a thrashing, combustible anxiety.

"Man," he said, "That's nothing to be thinking about, being a little late for work! That's small stuff. You should be devoting your brain to thinking about real things. Good things, things that will help you! See, I want to make fifteen thousand dollars today. And the job I'm in now, I can do it!

"I want to be a fashion designer, that's my goal. I use my brain for thinking about the things I want and making them happen. Wealth! Success! When I'm waiting for the bus home on Laurel Canyon, I stand at the newsstand there and I look at the fashion magazines—the trade magazines—and I picture myself in them. I imagine them talking about me, and I see my designs on the covers."

He held up his notebook.

"It's all right here; I write it all down, and I read it over and over again, so it's always the foremost thing on my mind. Wealth! Pleasure! Happiness! But I didn't always think like that. For many years of my life, I didn't focus on the things I needed to; but that's the way I was raised, the way my parents taught me.

"I don't blame my mother; she was just passing on what she had been taught. But I don't want to share those same things with *my* children. Wealth! Satisfaction! Achievement! Those are the kinds of things I want them to learn from me, the kinds of ideas I want them to grow up hearing."

The bus reached my stop, and I stood to go.

"Well, good luck," I told him. "I hope you make your fifteen thousand dollars today at work."

"Good luck to you! And I *will!*"

I said goodbye at Woodman. At the stop, I saw all the usual people I rode in with every morning were still waiting there. I took my place among them, and the driver pulled around the corner shortly after. She was ten minutes late, as usual.

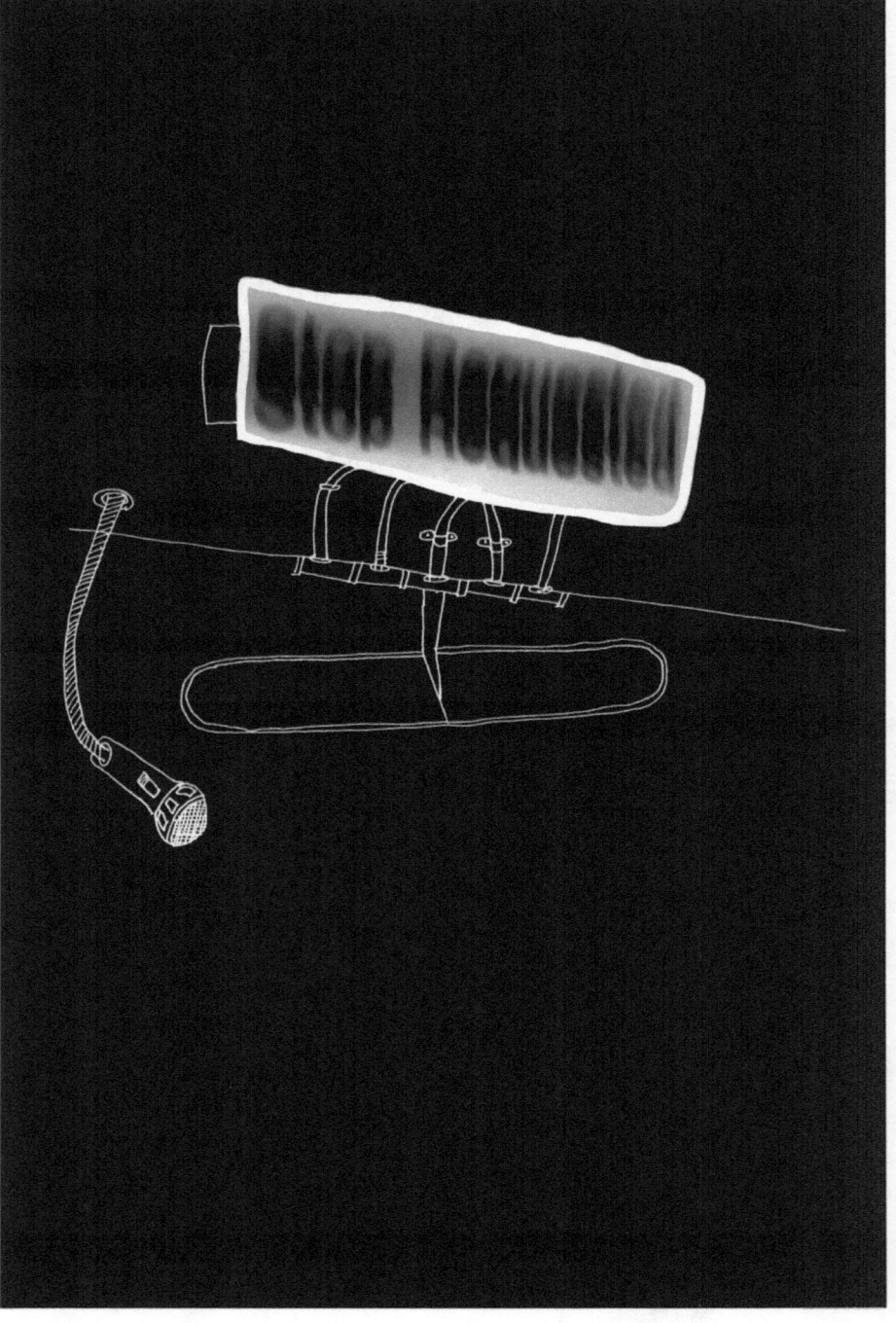

acknowledgements

This collection was Stanley Zappa's idea, and he's been an inspiring and generous collaborator. I'm proud to share this book with him.

I owe a lot to the beautiful and brilliant Sandee Curry. Not only for her expert and sympathetic copy editing, but also for her unflagging enthusiasm and constant support. She made everything easier, and still does.

Thank you Cormac Foster, Andy Biscontini, Paul Silva, Jason Cuadrado, Jeanne Arneberg, Robert Silva, Vic Nol, Vanina Marsot, Marjorie Sa'adah, Thomas Converse Bright, Duke Comby, Mark Leonard, Jeff Doyle, Albert Genna, Moby Pomerance, Peter Joshua Hoffman, Eric Reymond, Jason Lenzi, Josh Alan Friedman, Tonya Wise, Tom & Yuko Weisser, Lupé Carranza, Harlan Ellison, Ray Bradbury, Melvin Van Peebles, Innes Weir, Georgeanna Juliano, Carroll Juliano, Jonathan, Clayton, and Victoria.

With special thanks to James.

A founding contributor to the NewTexture.com website, WYATT DOYLE is the editor of Andrew Biscontini's *nu luna* and co-editor and designer of the collections *Weasels Ripped My Flesh!* (with Robert Deis and Josh Alan Friedman) and *He-Men, Bag Men & Nymphos* (with Deis) for New Texture. He is the editor of Josh Alan Friedman's *Black Cracker* for his own imprint. *I'm Here For You*, his original story and screenplay with Jason Cuadrado, has been adapted as the film *Devil May Call*.

I Need Real Tuxedo and a Top Hat!, a collection of his photographs and stories, is forthcoming from New Texture.

He lives in Los Angeles.

photo by Sandee Curry

MAN UP!

... For a shirt-ripping, gut-punching anthology showcasing two-fisted writing *ripped* from the pages of long-lost vintage men's adventure magazines of the 1950s, '60s and '70s ...

... For rare, bare-knuckle stories and reminiscences by some of the toughest writers ever to punch a typewriter ...

... For outrageous, *100% true* tales of **sex**, **crime**, **combat**, **jungle goddesses**, **beatnik girls**, **LSD experiments**, **animal attacks** and **nymphos**. Always **nymphos** ...

... For **WEASELS RIPPED MY FLESH!**

PREVIEW THE BOOK AT **WEASELSRIPPED**.COM

WEASELS RIPPED MY FLESH!

TWO-FISTED STORIES FROM MEN'S ADVENTURE MAGAZINES OF THE 1950s, '60s & '70s

featuring

LAWRENCE BLOCK

JANE DOLINGER

ROBERT F. DORR

HARLAN ELLISON

BRUCE JAY FRIEDMAN

WALTER KAYLIN

KEN KRIPPENE

MARIO PUZO

ROBERT SILVERBERG

WALTER WAGER

edited by
Robert Deis
with Josh Alan Friedman & Wyatt Doyle

Man's Life

SEPTEMBER 25¢

SIN HAPPY VACATIONISTS
ARE OVERRUNNING CAPE COD

HOOKED TO A KILLER SHARK

CAN WOMEN JUSTIFY THEIR NEED FOR
EXTRA-MARITAL RELATIONS?

MENSPULPMAGS.com   # new texture

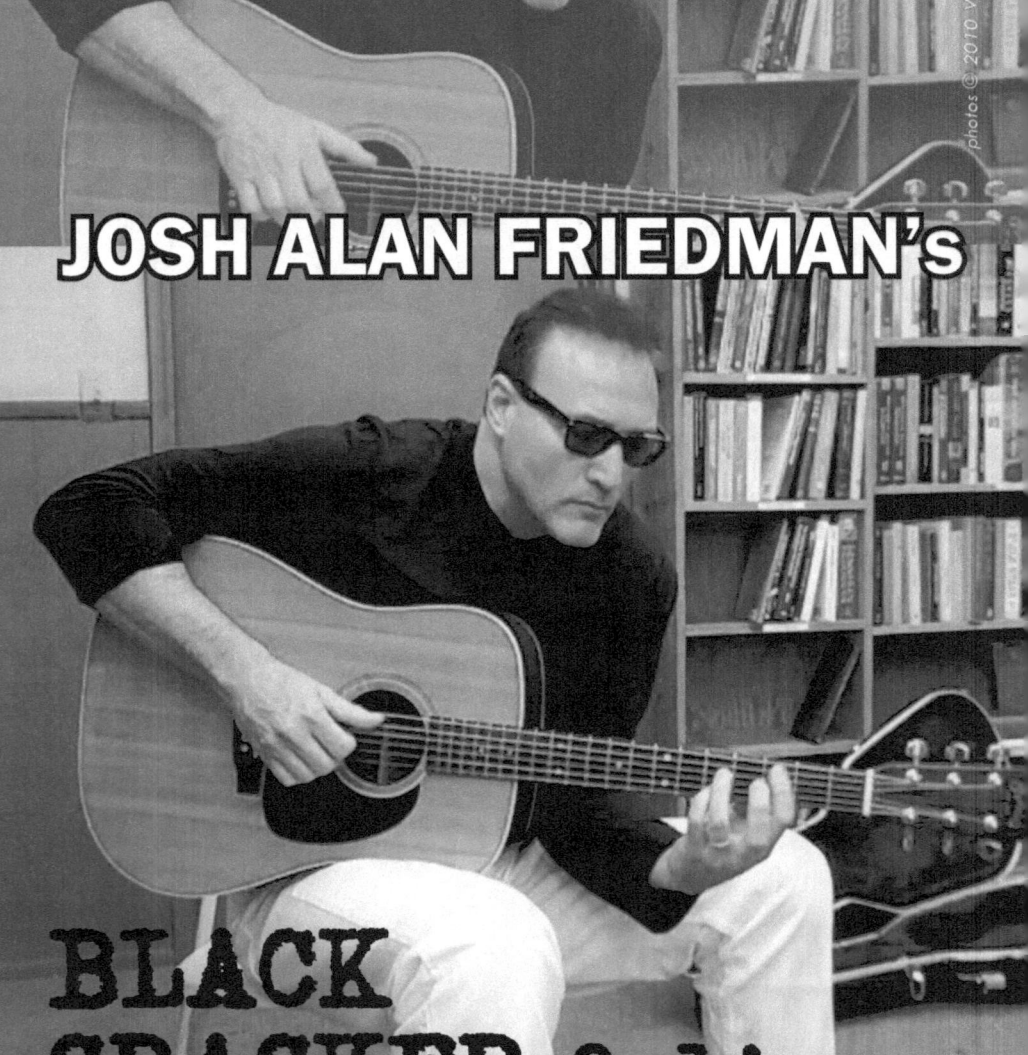

JOSH ALAN FRIEDMAN's

BLACK
CRACKER Online

music * video * archives * shop

[BlackCrackerOnline.com]

photos © 2010 Wyatt Doyle

1965. Flashpoint of the Civil Rights Movement.

In every American city, interracial tensions threaten to boil over into violence.

And in Glen Cove, Long Island, Josh Friedman finds himself on the front lines of the fight for racial equality.

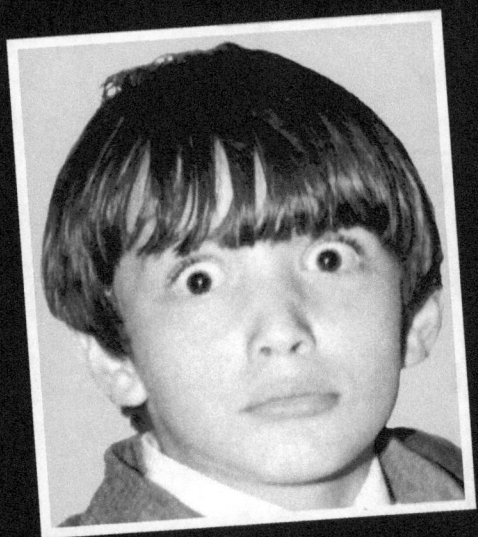

Josh is nine.

Race. Segregation. Doo-doo jokes.

BLACK CRACKER

an autobiographical novel
by Josh Alan Friedman

from 🦅 WYATT DOYLE BOOKS
www.BlackCrackerOnline.com

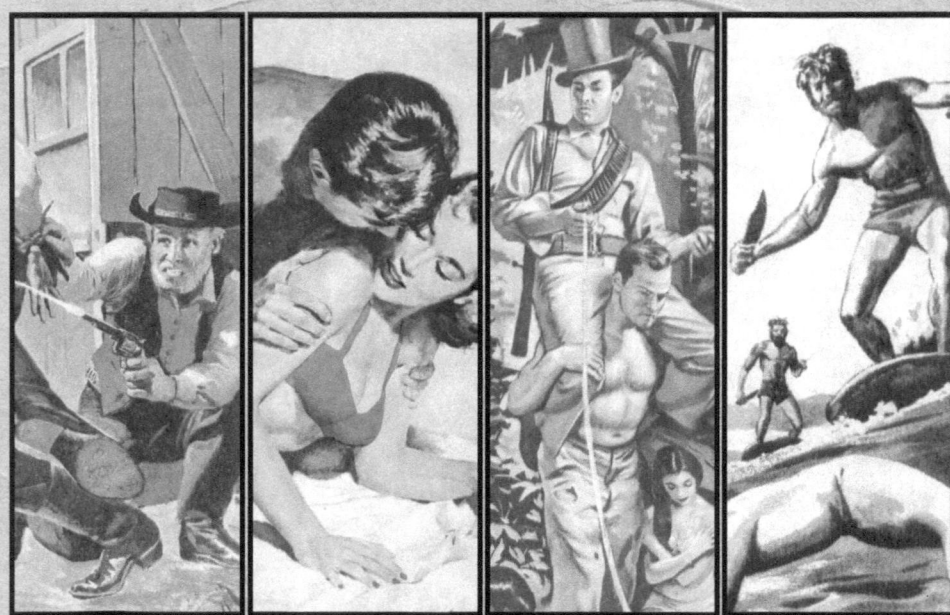

Gunfighters. Lovers. Kings. Surf Pack Assassins.

The World of
MEN'S ADVENTURE MAGAZINES'

Scores of great authors wrote for men's adventure pulps—**Elmore Leonard, Jim Thompson, Richard Matheson, Lawrence Block** and **Harlan Ellison**, to name a few. But the wordsmith writers for *Man's World* and *True Action* envied most was **Walter Kaylin**.

Leaving an indelible mark on three decades of sweat-soaked pulp fiction, Walter Kaylin tackled testosterone-fueled subjects from Westerns to war, secret agents to sex sirens, Nazis to *noir*. His frequently over-the-top plots and characters scaled new heights of ingenuity and invention, while setting the standard for the kind of unapologetic savagery and excess that made men's adventure magazines notorious—then and now.

Walter Kaylin's He-Men, Bag Men & Nymphos hits like a clenched fist; get yours or get out of the way!

edited by Robert Deis and Wyatt Doyle

Ladies' Men. He-Men. Bag Men. Nymphos.

WALTER KAYLIN

WILDEST WRITER

"Walter Kaylin, come back!"

— Mario Puzo,
author of *The Godfather*

original magazine illustrations by (from left): George Eisenberg, Don Neiser, Al Rossi, Earl Norem, Joe Little, Earl Norem, Samson Pollen, Gil Cohen

FROM THE MEN WHO BROUGHT YOU
WEASELS RIPPED MY FLESH!

HE-MEN, BAG MEN & NYMPHOS
classic men's adventure magazine stories by
WALTER KAYLIN
edited by Robert Deis and Wyatt Doyle

new texture | MENSPULPMAGS.com

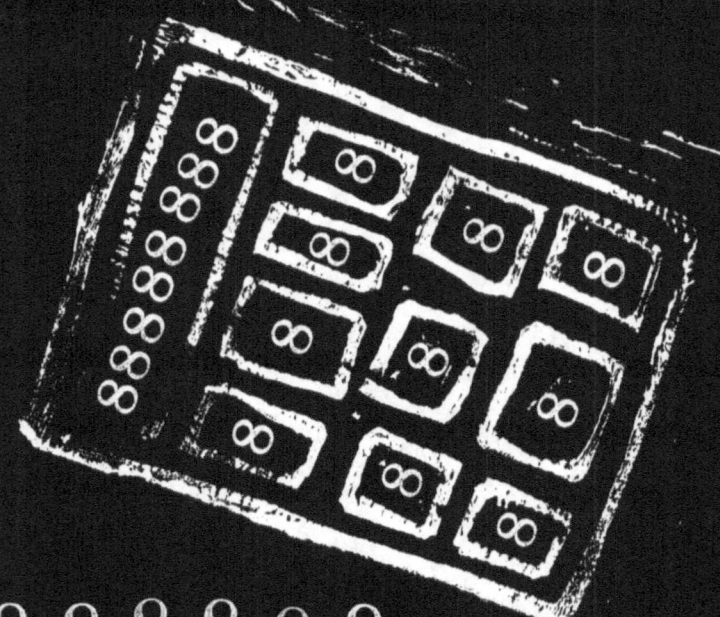

8 8 8 8 8 8 8

new
computer
music

by
stanley
j.
zappa

new texture

digital download and limited edition compact disc at cdbaby

"Bold, brusque and vibrant...this band makes a pressing claim for attention."

- Jerry D'Souza, *AllAboutJazz.com*

"If you're getting fed up of the tired New York and Chicago-based cliques of American free jazz, do yourself a favour and get a copy of this."

- Dan Warburton, *Paris Transatlantic*

Leonard, Skrowaczewski, Zappa
VISIONS

Mark Leonard - Acoustic Bass
Nick Skrowaczewski - Percussion
Stanley Jason Zappa - Tenor Saxophone, Bb Clarinet

Cover painting by Bill Dixon

ARCHIVE/EDITION
110 1971 4

available on compact disc and digital download from

"YOU ARE SO COMFORTABLE WITH A PLACE — A SUBWAY STATION, SAY — THAT YOU FEEL LIKE IT IS YOURS. You know its details by heart and can pace down its platforms in your mind. You know its color, its shade of green, the nicks and bruises of its pillars, the grime and putrid smells, the buttons of filth that cake the tiles, the slight descent of the cement platform as it nears the walls and the diameter of the pipe holes that peak from the base of the walls. You feel you might be entitled to bring down your sofa from your apartment, if you had the gumption, and set it up right on the platform and kick your feet up. You feel that you are entitled to lounge on the benches, stretch out if you are alone, perhaps walk around in your socks. You can belch and fart and blow your nose. It is an extension of your foyer.

"YET, IT IS NOT YOURS. For it also belongs to 10,000 others, the population of a medium-sized North Eastern town, a Bennington or a Brattleboro, say, a population that waits alongside you for the train and fumes and waits for the train and fumes. And you wonder what they think about the station. Do they claim it as their own? Would they fight you for it? You wonder."

ERIC REYMOND
VOLUMES OF WORLDS: ESSAYS ON BROOKYN, KANSAS AND BEYOND

Volumes of Worlds:
Essays on Brooklyn, Kansas, and Beyond.

Eric Reymond

new texture

The future is beautiful
and dangerous.

photo © 2013 Wyatt Doyle

n u l u n a

Andrew Biscontini

nu luna

a novel by Andrew Biscontini

www.nulunaverse.com

new texture

This is
Reverend
Branch.

Services are underway
at RevBranch.com

photo © 2011 Wyatt Doyle

BOOKSELLERS

most
New Texture
releases
are available
through
Ingram

WOODEN PEN

Fuck

photos © 2010 Wyatt Doyle

#newtexture.com

www.ingramcontent.com/pod-product-compliance
Lightning Source LLC
Chambersburg PA
CBHW051301250626
47155CB00009B/3381